"I should have told you about Mandy," Scott said.

"Why didn't you?" Lori said.

"I don't know. It's hard to talk about her, especially when Joey is listening."

"I'm sorry you lost someone you loved."

"I don't want sympathy. I mean, it was more than three years ago. My son and I have moved on."

Scott wondered if she could ever understand. It was tempting to pour out all his feelings. Lori was the best listener he'd ever known, but sometimes words weren't enough.

Joey yelled out to him, and Scott followed Lori to the edge of the sandbox. Scott bent down to brush some sand off his son's hair. Lori said goodbye to them and started walking home alone.

He watched her disappear from sight. Every instinct urged him to go after her, but even if he caught up, what then? He had nothing to offer her. He'd loved her once, or so he thought. Could they even think about a future together?

PAM ANDREWS

is the mother-daughter writing team of Pam Hanson
and Barbara Andrews. Barbara makes her home with
Pam and her family in Nebraska. They have written
numerous books for such publishers as Steeple
Hill Books and Guideposts. Pam's background is
in journalism, and she and her college-professor
husband have two sons. Barbara, the mother of four
and grandmother of seven, also writes articles and a
column about collectible postcards.

Hometown Reunion
Pam Andrews

Steeple
Hill®

Published by Steeple Hill Books™

STEEPLE HILL BOOKS

Steeple
Hill®

Recycling programs
for this product may
not exist in your area.

ISBN-13: 978-0-373-87552-8

HOMETOWN REUNION

Copyright © 2009 by Pamela Hanson and Barbara Andrews

www.SteepleHill.com

Printed in U.S.A.

After all, every house is built by someone,
but God is the builder of everything.
—*Hebrews* 3:4

To friends, near and far.

Chapter One

Scott Mara started walking toward his pickup, holding the small, damp hand of his four-year-old son, Joey. He was about to open the door and boost him up to his car seat when he caught a glimpse of a woman walking toward him on the sidewalk. At first he paid no attention, anxious to finish his errands and get to Joey's dental appointment. As a single father, he was hard-pressed to keep up with all his son's needs, especially those that kept him from work, but he was a little worried about one of Joey's baby teeth, wondering if it should be pulled to make room for the new one bulging in his jaw.

The woman had to be a stranger in town. He had lived in Apple Grove, Iowa, all his life and knew everyone by sight, if not by name. Still, there was something familiar about her. Maybe his eyes were playing tricks, because she reminded him of someone he'd known a long time ago.

She started to cross the street, and he impulsively scooped up his son to cut her off on the other side. It was unlikely that Lori Raymond was back in town, but his curiosity got the best of him.

"Daddy, I can walk," Joey noisily protested.

"Sure you can," he said, depositing him on the sidewalk a few yards in front of the woman.

"Scott!"

It was a voice that made his spine tingle.

"I almost didn't recognize you," she said.

He pulled off his straw Western-style hat and kept one hand on Joey's shoulder so he wouldn't wander off.

"Lori, I'm surprised to see you here."

"I'm visiting my aunt."

"Of course," he said, feeling awkward because he hadn't immediately connected her to Bess Raymond.

"How've you been?" she asked.

It was the kind of casual question people asked each other all the time, but coming from her, it made him want to answer honestly.

Instead he said, "Fine. How about you?"

"Good, although I've gotten myself in something of a predicament."

"Oh?"

Joey was squirming. Scott knew that he should cut the conversation short and get to the dentist, but Lori used to be his favorite person to talk to.

"Aunt Bess has drafted me to help restart the Highway Café. I keep telling her that I won't be here long, but you know how she is."

She still had the same mischievous little grin, and when she looked up at him, he remembered how she'd always made him feel better about himself.

"I sure do." He smiled, recalling how his favorite

teacher, Lori's aunt, could put him in his place when he deserved it. "You're on vacation from your job?" He knew it was none of his business, but he'd often wondered what had become of her after high school, if she'd gotten married, had a family.

"Afraid not. I came to a parting of the ways with the head chef at the restaurant where I was working. I've been offered a job in a new restaurant that's opening after Labor Day, if I decide to go back to Chicago. What about you? I saw you coming out of the hardware store. You always did like building things. Are you doing it for a living now?"

"Daddy!"

"Sorry, I'm forgetting my manners. This is my son, Joey. Joey, this is Miss Raymond—it is still Miss, isn't it?"

She bent and offered her hand to his son. Much to his father's satisfaction, Joey responded with grave courtesy.

"I'm so happy to meet you, Joey. You can call me Lori." She smiled and straightened. "And it is still Miss."

He wanted to say that the men in Chicago must be blind to let her slip away, but he squelched the impulse. It had been nearly ten years since he'd last seen her. He remembered her question and gave the shortest possible answer.

"I have my own contracting business, but most of the time, I'm the only employee."

"Somehow I didn't expect…"

She trailed off, uncertain how much she should say, but he could guess. She hadn't expected him to stay in Apple Grove.

Some things were best left unsaid.

"You look good, Lori." It sounded lame, but it was all he could think of saying.

What a feeble compliment, he thought. She looked

terrific. Her dark brown eyes sparkled. Her cheeks were rosy, and her thick chestnut curls were spilling out of a ponytail, the way they had in high school. He'd been a fool not to tell her how he'd felt about her back then, but the gulf between them had been too wide. He didn't want to think about how different his life might be if he hadn't been constrained by her strong faith, one he couldn't share.

"Daddy, we're going to be late!"

Joey impatiently tugged on his pant leg. If there was one thing his son hated, it was being late.

"We're on our way to the dentist," Scott explained. "It's been nice seeing you, Lori. I hope you enjoy your time here."

"Thanks, Scott. It is good to be back."

As soon as Joey was settled into his car seat, Scott started thinking of all the questions he should have asked. But maybe it was for the best. He and Lori had taken different forks in the road. He had too much on his plate to torment himself with what might have been.

Lori spent the time before her aunt came home from school organizing the cheerful second-floor bedroom that had always been her home away from home, but her mind wasn't on the task of unpacking. She'd been so surprised at seeing Scott again that she hadn't asked any of the things she wanted to know. Had he married someone she knew? Did they have other children? Why did Scott decide to stay in Apple Grove? Surely he could have found better opportunities in a larger town.

She couldn't get him out of her mind as she filled drawers lined with tissue paper and hung the rest of her clothes in the closet. He'd never been what high school girls called cute, but his clear blue eyes and high cheek-bones made his face memorable. Now, at twenty-nine, two years older than her, he had a brooding quality that made her want to know if everything was well with him.

She went through her unpacking absentmindedly, her thoughts focused on the brief meeting with Scott. It didn't take her long to finish, since she'd never been a person to accumulate a lot of possessions or a large wardrobe. She'd brought her chef's knives, still in the trunk of her car, and a good supply of work clothes, but it hadn't been worthwhile to move her well-worn sec-ondhand furniture from the suburban Chicago apart-ment she'd been sharing with a friend. She'd offered first choice to her recently married ex-roommate and donated the rest to a charity shop.

When she'd done all that could be done, she sat on the edge of the bed and caught a glimpse of her image in the full-length gilt-framed mirror mounted on the wall. The face that looked back at her was weary. Her dark brown eyes were shadowed, and her chestnut mane had grown into an untamed mass of curls. She hadn't bothered with makeup since that awful day when she'd rashly walked out of Arcadia, the posh Chicago restau-rant where she'd been working.

Maybe she'd set her sights too high, but she'd been thrilled when she was hired by Gardner Knolls as an ap-prentice chef at one of his three Windy City restaurants. She'd expected to start at the bottom, and that meant doing all the menial chores, from chopping vegetables to taking inventory in the freezer.

The trouble was, she'd started at the bottom and stayed

at the bottom, while chefs with less talent were regularly promoted. When Adrian, a klutzy young man of meager talent and four years her junior, was given charge of the luncheon service, she realized that the head chef would never let her realize her potential. He had trained in Paris and looked down his nose at her small town Iowa origins, sneering at her for winning county-fair blue ribbons.

She didn't regret quitting on the spot, but now the question was, should she say yes to the job offer she had? It might be hard to find anything better since she wasn't likely to get a good reference after walking out without giving notice. But could she afford to stay in Chicago without a roommate to share expenses?

Lori wanted to consider the new job offer calmly and logically, but it was her nature to crave the rush of excitement that came with being pushed to the maximum. It was what she loved most about being a chef, creating wonderful dishes under pressure. She felt at loose ends, and neither her aunt nor her parents could help her find her way. Only the Lord could give her the guidance she so badly needed.

"Dear Lord," she prayed, sitting on the edge of the bed, with her head bowed, "help me to forgive those who have wronged me and to accept responsibility for my own bad decisions. Please show me a way to serve You and use the talents You've given me. I thank You for having so richly blessed my life."

She squeezed her hands together, willing herself to find forgiveness in her heart for the way the head chef had treated her, but it was exceedingly hard. There was a void in her heart, and she'd let it fill up with anger.

Maybe a short stay in Apple Grove would give her

time to put things in perspective. She needed to recover not only her self-confidence but her commitment to excel in her career. She loved making people happy with cuisine that was not only wonderful tasting but good for them, as well.

Her thoughts strayed to her chance meeting with Scott. No one had been more eager to leave town than he had, yet he'd stayed and was raising a son here. Sometimes life was a puzzle, and she didn't begin to have all the answers.

By the time Aunt Bess got home from school, Lori had showered and dressed in white walking shorts and a bright peach tank top. It was warm for May, and she was glad to change out of her jeans and polo shirt.

"My, don't you look sweet," Bess said when she saw her niece. "But you didn't need to change for Carl and me."

"Carl?"

"Oh, I've been so excited about you being here, I forgot to tell you. We're meeting Carl Mitchell at the café after dinner to go over some things that need doing. He promised the electricity would be on by then. Guess we should be able to rely on him since he worked for the power company for forty-two years before he retired. Now he has plenty of free time to help get the café back on track."

"So he's one of the twenty-four people who bought the café?"

It boggled her mind that so many people had banded together to reopen the Highway Café after it had been closed for over a year. When it looked as if no one would buy it, her aunt had spearheaded a campaign to have a committee buy it. The town was suffering without a place where people could congregate and get a good meal.

"Him, me and twenty-two others," her aunt said with a soft chuckle. "But don't worry. None of us know beans about running a restaurant. We'll do things your way."

"I hope you've told your committee that I'll only be here a little while, just long enough to get things started and help you hire permanent help."

"I haven't told them yet, but I'll be sure to mention it at our next meeting," Bess promised. "Now, I have two TV dinners. Would you like turkey with stuffing or roast beef with mashed potatoes?"

Lori quietly sighed at her aunt's comment about not telling the committee yet, but she didn't say anything about it.

"Either is fine. I'll put them in the microwave for you."

The last time her aunt had tried to cook frozen dinners, she'd mistakenly used the regular oven directions and microwaved an entrée to the consistency of shoe leather.

"Would you mind? I'll just slip into some old clothes. Last time I was there, I couldn't help but notice how dusty the café is, but don't worry about the dirt. We have lots of volunteers for the cleanup."

Her aunt soon returned, her rust-colored, gray-streaked hair covered by a little flowered bandana. She was wearing faded jeans and a yellow-and-brown striped smock that went nearly to her knees, a drastic change from the sedate navy, forest-green and burgundy dresses she favored for teaching.

Lori made a show of eating some of the bland turkey

dinner, but she needn't have bothered. Bess was so excited about the café that she scarcely noticed her niece's lack of appetite.

Bess still lived in the yellow frame house on Second Avenue that she'd inherited from her parents. From the front porch, Lori could get a glimpse of the church steeple, and it brought back happy memories of Sunday school, church picnics and the fellowship of the congregation. She was looking forward to meeting the new minister on Sunday, although she regretted that Reverend Green wouldn't be there. He'd finally taken a much-deserved retirement.

"I saw Scott Mara when I took a walk around town," Lori said, trying to sound casual.

"Scott was such a little rascal when he was in my class," Bess said as she bustled around the kitchen, cleaning up their hasty dinner. "He was always the town bad boy, but he had a sweet nature for all that. Oh, dear, we'd better hurry. Carl will be waiting for us."

They elected to walk since it was only a few blocks, crossing Beech Street and approaching the café from the rear. The back door was padlocked, forcing them to cut between buildings to the Main Street entrance.

"Oh, good! The lights are on," Bess said. "Now you can get a better idea of what needs to be done."

A faded blue pickup like the one Scott had driven was parked at an angle in front of the café. Of course, there were probably a hundred like it in the county, but she couldn't help wondering whether she would see him again while she was in town.

"Come on in, ladies." A portly man with a white

beard and a matching mane of hair opened the front door and motioned them inside.

"This is my niece," Bess said. "Lori, Carl Mitchell is the man who's going to help us put this place in order."

"Not by myself, I'm not," he said, with a belly-shaking laugh. "That's why Scott is here."

Carl gestured at the man who was stooped down, examining the front of the lunch counter, with a small boy beside him. He slowly rose, straightening to his full six feet two inches, exactly ten inches taller than Lori. It was easier for her to remember this than to look directly into his eyes.

"Scott, this is Bessie's niece—"

Scott nodded. "Yes, I saw Lori in town earlier."

"Scott, I didn't expect to see you here." Lori's voice didn't sound as though it belonged to her.

"Oh, you two know each other," Carl said. "Splendid, since you'll be working together until we get this place fixed up."

"Scott runs his own construction company," Bess said. "He did some wonderful work at the school, so I know he'll take care of everything that needs doing around here."

"Hi, Lori," Joey said.

Lori was enchanted when the little boy remembered her name and offered his hand for a very adult shake.

"Lori has agreed to be our chief cook and manager," Bess said.

"Only until the café is up and running," Lori added so quickly that the words came out sounding breathless.

"I'd like to say that the place will be ready for business in a few weeks, but from what I've seen so far, there's quite a bit to be done to get it up to code," Scott said. "I'm going to have to rip out the wainscoting to see what's underneath, and that window will fall out of the frame if someone blows hard."

"You're making it sound expensive," Carl said, his laugh not quite so hearty now.

"I'll give you the best deal I can," Scott said, speaking to the older man but looking in Lori's direction. "First, I'll have to check out the basement and roof, but it's the kitchen that really worries me. I don't know how they ever got a gas range that big and heavy into the place."

"Old Amos Conklin was real proud of that monstrosity," Carl said, talking about the café's longtime owner. "Wouldn't surprise me if he took out the front window to get it in."

"Yeah, that would work since you've got double swinging doors going into the kitchen. If it were up to me, though, I'd sell it for scrap metal." Scott shook his head, and his eyes met Lori's. "How does that sound to you?" he asked her.

Lori looked around the dusky interior of the old kitchen with misgivings. The café had been in the same family for three generations, and the gas range looked to be as old as the original owner.

"It's not a decision I can make," she said tactfully. "I'm only temporary help."

"Of course, you can, Lori. You know much more about running a kitchen than anyone on the committee," her aunt said.

"I think I can speak for everyone," Carl said. "Whatever works for you is fine with us. We planned on making some big improvements when we pooled our money to buy it. We're hoping you'll work with Scott on this."

"I really don't know anything about renovations," Lori replied.

"Maybe not, but you know how a restaurant should be. I think it's a splendid idea for you to consult with Scott," Bess said.

"Splendid," Lori repeated in an unsure voice.

"I can't do anything until Monday," Scott said. "I have to finish a wheelchair ramp this weekend so the home owner can come home from a nursing home. Why don't you meet me here Monday morning, after I drop Joey off at day care. Make it about eight-fifteen."

Scott scooped up his son, said his goodbyes and headed for the door.

Her aunt beamed, Carl smiled benevolently and Lori felt as if she'd just stepped into quicksand. She wanted to do this favor for her aunt as quickly as possible and get on with her life somewhere else. Scott was the one person in Apple Grove who could awaken old feelings and complicate her life.

What had she gotten herself into?

Chapter Two

Anyone who thought small-town life was too quiet should follow Aunt Bess around for a day, Lori thought.

She was pretending to read a book she'd borrowed from her aunt's bookcase, but the words were a meaningless jumble as she thought about the prospect of working with Scott.

"Just one more phone call," Bess called out from the kitchen. "Then we'll have a little chat before bed."

Lori knew that her aunt was eager to hear all the details about her departure from the job in Chicago, but she wasn't ready to release all the pain bottled up inside of her. Bess would see her point of view and envelop her in sympathy. She would counsel her to put her faith in the Lord and would tell her everything would work out for the best. Lori wholeheartedly wanted to believe that, but she wasn't ready to share her frustration and loss of confidence, not even with her dear aunt.

"I know you and Scott will work well together," Bess said, plopping down in her recliner and using her toes to kick off her sandals. "I remember how you always dropped by when he was scheduled to cut my grass. When you were here, he took double the time to do my yard. Seeing as how you both had such big crushes, I was surprised that you never dated."

Lori blushed. Had she and Scott been so transparent with their feelings back then?

"Well, it looks like you could use a good night's sleep," Bess said. "I hate to admit it, but I'm worn to a frazzle, what with the field trip my class is planning and all the business with the café. I think I'll go to bed. Is there anything you need?"

"No, I'm fine."

"Well, I'll say good-night, then. I'm so happy the Lord has brought you home to Apple Grove."

"I'm grateful to be here. Thank you for taking me in."

"As if I don't love you like a daughter," her aunt said, giving her a hug.

For a few moments after Bess left the room, Lori basked in the warmth of her aunt's love. She adored Bess, and she hated the thought of disappointing her when it came time to leave.

Monday morning Scott gave Joey's face a quick once-over with the washcloth, satisfied that his milk mustache and the stray bits of oatmeal were gone. He might only be imagining it, but the women at the day care seemed to inspect his son with eagle eyes whenever Scott dropped him off. They didn't seem to trust a single father to keep his child neat and clean. It wasn't easy, but he loved Joey, and would do all he could to raise him right.

"Can I take my yo-yo?"

"Better not. We'll have another lesson after supper."

Joey was showing amazing dexterity with his hands, and Scott was proud that his son was taking after him that way, if not in appearance. He had pale blond hair and bright blue eyes, not unlike Scott's in childhood, but his heart-shaped face was nothing like his father's. Scott could still see Mandy's face etched on their son's.

"I hope we don't have that soup with things in it," Joey said as he followed his father to the pickup. "I hate vegables."

"Vegetables," Scott corrected absentmindedly. "Climb up, big guy."

It was a short drive from the trailer park to the day-care center. He'd tried leaving Joey with a neighbor, but the woman had been more interested in her three poodles than his son. When he'd learned that Joey hardly ever got to play outside, he'd immediately enrolled him in group care. It was more expensive, something he could barely afford since his business gave him a decent living but not much for extras.

He parked in front of the neat brick house and went around to the back entrance that led to the lower level, which had been converted into space for preschool children.

As usual, one of the helpers gave Joey a warm welcome when they went inside and immediately steered him to a play station.

"Did you bring the form for our trip to the farm?" Betty Drummond, the head caregiver, asked Scott.

He'd flunked parenthood again. The pink slip of paper was at home, on the kitchen counter.

"Would it be all right if I drop it off when I pick Joey up?"

Betty had a round, friendly face framed by fluffy silver hair, but her silence told him that it wasn't all right.

"The children are really looking forward to their trip to the farm," she said.

"I'll run home and get it," he said, wondering why she didn't have an extra form he could sign there. Surely he wasn't the only parent who ever forgot.

"I'd appreciate it," Betty said cordially enough, although no doubt her thoughts weren't as understanding as her voice. Didn't moms ever make mistakes?

He returned to the aging white-and-green trailer he called home and hurriedly filled in the blanks on the field-trip form. He couldn't fault the day care for wanting a doctor's name and an emergency number, but the closest person he had as a contact person was his sister, Doreen, and she lived nearly forty miles away.

His parents were even farther away, since his father had had to move west to Omaha to find a job when Apple Grove's only plant had closed. He'd worked his way up to foreman of the milk-processing facility, and it had been a blow to lose the only employer he'd ever had as an adult. Now his dad was counting the months until he could afford to retire from a tedious night watchman job.

All the friends he and Mandy had had as a couple had dropped out of sight, too. Most likely it was his fault. Taking care of Joey and trying to make a living took all his time and energy.

By the time he delivered the permission form, he was late for his appointment at the old café. He'd made a few rough sketches and done some estimates to show the committee, but he had a lot more work to do before he could make a final bid for the project. He never would've dreamed he'd be working with Lori Raymond. He still marveled that she was back in Apple Grove.

He drove the short distance to Main Street and parked in front of the café. Ten years ago he would have done anything for a chance to be alone with Lori, but she'd been a good girl in every sense of the word. Everything she'd said and done had sent him a message: She wouldn't have anything to do with a wild kid who didn't embrace churchgoing.

He felt differently about a lot of things now, even taking Joey to Sunday school every week, but he still didn't feel comfortable in church or feel God played a part in his life. He'd had to grow up fast when Mandy died, but part of him still felt like the rebellious outcast. The town accepted him for his construction skills, but he never felt like he belonged.

The lights showed dimly through the filthy front window, so he guessed Lori was in the café, waiting for him. He couldn't believe it, but he actually felt a little nervous about seeing her again.

Scott was late.

Lori hoped nothing was wrong and knew it was her own worries about her future that were making her impatient. She certainly didn't want to get off to a bad start with Scott by mentioning his tardiness. The sooner he could get the café ready to open, the sooner she could leave to take a permanent job.

"Hello!"

She heard him calling from the front and went out to meet him.

"Good morning," she said, surprised that she felt a little breathless seeing him again.

"Sorry I'm late." He didn't explain why.

"I was just looking around. It looks worse in the daylight."

He laughed. "I think they'd be better off building a new place on the outskirts of town, but that isn't what they want."

"No, my aunt made it plain that they're hoping to revive Main Street."

"I thought they'd have trouble getting a cook. A lot of the people who used to live here are gone."

"But you're still here," she blurted out, immediately wishing she could take the words back.

She'd vowed to avoid personal comments. After all, Scott didn't know that she'd lived for a glimpse of him all through high school. Whenever he had spoken to her, she'd recorded every word he'd said in her diary. But she wasn't a teenager with a crush anymore, and she didn't expect them to be more than casual acquaintances in the short time she'd be in town.

"Fate is funny sometimes," he said, looking around the dining area, with a little frown. "Do you want to keep the lunch counter or tear it out for more table room?"

"I don't have a strong opinion either way. I'm more interested in the kitchen," she said. Talking about the café renovations was much safer than dwelling on the past.

"I have a feeling the committee wants things just the way they've always been."

"You're probably right. My aunt hasn't talked to me

about finances, but she seems to think a few nails and a little cleaning will make it as good as new."

He laughed softly and took off the battered cowboy hat. His hair was a darker blond than she remembered, and tiny wrinkle lines radiated from the corners of his serious blue eyes. Still, ten years had made him even more handsome, and she imagined that he was a favorite with all the women in town.

"I have to check out the cellar and the roof, and I'll take a look at the wiring and plumbing. Hopefully, I won't find anything really bad, but the pharmacy down the street was riddled with termites a few years back. I had to shore up the whole building after the exterminators were done. I'm hoping that won't be necessary here, but this building is about a hundred years old."

"That doesn't sound good." She exhaled slowly and realized she'd been holding her breath.

"I wish they would've called me to do an inspection before they bought the building. Most buyers have one before they agree to a sale, but the folks here were too eager to restart the café."

"That would be my aunt," she said, with a little laugh. "I have a feeling she spearheaded the whole idea."

"Where do you want to start?"

"Oh." She was a bit surprised that he wanted her to give directions. "The kitchen, I guess."

"Thought any more about junking that monstrosity?"

"The range? I guess it depends on whether the committee wants to buy a new one."

The kitchen seemed even smaller with Scott taking up much of the room between the huge range and the work counter.

"My aunt has plenty of volunteers for the cleanup. I imagine they can haul away the debris and such."

He nodded absentmindedly. "It's an awkward setup, the waitress having to come through the swinging doors to deliver the food. You could take down part of this wall to make a pass-through for orders."

"That sounds expensive, tearing out a wall."

"The whole place needs new wallboard. That knotty pine wainscoting has to go, not to mention that the wallpaper above it is filthy and peeling off. I've no idea what I'll find when I've stripped it."

"I don't think the fridge is working," she said, remembering one of her big concerns. "It was turned on when the electricity came on last night, but it's still warm inside."

He only grunted. "Let's take a look at the cellar."

Did he mean for her to go down there with him? She'd never liked cellars, and she was afraid this one would be particularly creepy.

"I'm not so sure about this," she weakly protested.

"Follow me, and hang on to the railing. I don't trust these old steps."

He stepped through a door and felt with his hand for a light switch. When the light at the bottom of the steps went on, he still needed his flashlight. The single weak bulb dangling from a cord did little to illuminate the low-ceilinged cellar.

"Watch your head," he called back, stooping to avoid hitting his.

Lori crept close to him, relieved that at least she could stand upright.

"They never threw anything away," Scott said, sounding surprised as his light played over the shelves lining every wall. "Look at those tins. I bet that peanut butter pail is almost as old as the building."

Her curiosity made her forget how much she hated cellars. Apparently generations of the Conklin family hadn't believed in throwing anything away. She pointed at a red metal box.

"What on earth is that?"

"Probably a dispenser," he replied. "I imagine it sat on the lunch counter so a customer could put in a penny and get a box of matches."

"Look. Glass ketchup bottles. The labels are still on."

"At least they washed them," Scott said, without enthusiasm.

He was creeping around in the darkest corners at the far end of the cellar, moving his light over a foundation made of stones cemented together. She'd had enough.

"I'm going upstairs," she called out.

One thing he could put on his list was a new stairway with a railing that didn't shake when she touched it. But then, it was unlikely she'd be going down here very often. She would find other places to store supplies, even if they had to hang from the ceiling.

Scott was gone so long, she began to wonder whether she should call down or, worse, go looking for him. When he did emerge, his hands were black with grime.

"Do you mind if I wash up?" he asked.

"No, and by the way, you have a spiderweb in your hair."

She reached up and attempted to pull it away; she was sorry about her impulsive gesture when he looked at her with surprise. The nasty little strands stuck to her fingers, reminding her of how much she didn't like spiders. And how much she had liked Scott.

When he brought an extension ladder from his truck and propped it against the building, she elected not to follow him up to the roof. Whatever he found, she would have to take it on trust.

Aunt Bess and her committee must think highly of Scott, she decided, because he was the only one giving them an estimate on the work. Of course, her aunt thought the best of everyone.

The aluminum ladder was probably stronger than it looked, but it wobbled as Scott climbed up. He disappeared from sight for what seemed like a long time, and when he threw his leg over to climb down, she was even more nervous for him. She automatically said a prayer that he would get to the ground safely, then wondered whether he would scoff at her if he knew. The boy she'd been head over heels for seemed less cynical as an adult, but Lori wasn't sure.

"Bad news and good news," he said when he got to the ground. "The roof was tarred fairly recently. I think it's good for now, but the chimney needs some work."

"Can you do that, too?" she asked, wondering what the extent of his skill was.

"I can repair it, but I recommend a professional cleaning. The furnace was converted from coal. I suspect they may once have burned trash in it, too."

They'd burned coal? She had never known anyone who had a coal furnace. She was beginning to realize what a tremendous responsibility her aunt and the committee had undertaken in buying such an old building.

She didn't try to oversee the rest of his inspection.

Some things she could see for herself: the poor layout of the kitchen, the shabby condition of the linoleum flooring throughout the building, the urgent need to repaint the old-fashioned tin ceiling and the peeling surfaces of chairs that had probably been painted half a dozen different colors over the years.

"Wow," she said, more to herself than to him.

If it was God's plan to give her a tremendous challenge, He'd brought her to the right place. She would give it her all, but she still fervently hoped that she could accomplish what was needed and get on with her life as soon as possible.

After what seemed like hours of peeking, poking and probing, Scott sat across from her at one of the dusty tables.

"It will take me a while to work out everything that's needed and give you an estimate," he said, still writing figures on a pad.

"I understand."

He was all business, and she missed the easy friendship they'd had many years ago. She wanted to ask him about his life. Was he happy? Where was his wife? He'd yet to mention her, and she didn't want to pry. She didn't know where he lived or why he seemed to take sole responsibility for Joey. But nothing he said or did invited the kind of confidences they'd once shared.

When he'd said everything there was to say about the renovation, he slipped his notepad into the back pocket of his jeans and retrieved his hat.

He turned at the doorway with a twinkle in his eyes that she hadn't seen in a long time.

"When you cook, do you wear one of those chef's hats?" He sketched a tall shape in the air with his hands.

"It depends on where I'm working."

"Here, for instance."

"I suppose I could. Why do you ask?" She eyed him quizzically.

"Just wondering how you'd look in a starchy white getup."

He grinned and was gone.

Chapter Three

Lori punched in numbers on her cell phone, looking forward to a long chat with her best friend from high school, Sara Bennings. They'd kept in touch via e-mail, but actually getting together in person was a treat and one of the benefits of spending the summer in Apple Grove. Sara had married her high school boyfriend and settled into life as a farmer's wife and the mother of Sunny, her four-year-old daughter.

"Hi. It's me, Lori," she said when Sara answered.

She was rewarded by a squeal of pleasure, and she could almost see her excitable, red-haired friend go pink-cheeked with enthusiasm.

"What are you going to be doing all summer, until the café is ready to open?" Sara asked after they exchanged recent news.

"A woman I know is writing a cookbook of recipes that will appeal to preschoolers. She's going to pay me to test some of them while I'm here."

"That sounds like fun."

"I expect it will be, and it will give me a little income before I take another restaurant job."

"Any prospects?" Sara asked. "I hate to think of you leaving again, but I can't imagine any jobs around here that would interest you."

"One with good potential in Chicago, but I don't need to make up my mind right away. The restaurant is still under construction."

They had so much to catch up on that Lori was surprised to see that they'd been talking for over an hour. She said goodbye, promising that they'd get together soon.

One thing she hadn't mentioned to her friend was working with Scott on the café. Sara was the only friend who'd known about Lori's big crush on him in high school. Sara might get the wrong idea if Lori brought it up. Lori didn't want her friend to think she was still attracted to Scott after all this time. He was, after all, a married man.

"Daddy, wake up!"

Scott reluctantly opened one eye and grimaced at his son.

"How about letting me sleep a few more minutes?" he asked.

"You said we'd do something fun today," Joey reminded him, planting himself astride Scott's chest and digging in with his knees.

"What time is it?" He turned his head to look at the big red numbers on his alarm. "Seven o'clock! You don't get up this early on day-care days."

He couldn't help noticing that Joey was already dressed in jeans and a green T-shirt, with the tag sticking out in front.

"I don't have to go there today. Get up, Daddy!"

"I will if you get off me."

Scott ruffled his son's fine blond hair and growled in an imitation of a tiger. Joey tumbled off the edge of the bed and slipped his feet into the big work boots sitting on the floor. Scott reluctantly sat up while his son clunked the short distance to the kitchen area. Scott slept on a hide-a-bed in the trailer's living area so Joey could have the only partitioned bedroom. It gave his son a private place where he could keep his toys, although they still seemed to spill out all over the place.

Scott stood, his foot narrowly missing a plastic dinosaur. He really should make Joey pick up all his toys before he went to bed at night, but sometimes they were both too tired.

Joey was rummaging in a lower cupboard, where they kept the cereal and crackers.

"I'll make you some oatmeal as soon as I get dressed," Scott said. "Meanwhile, pick up your toys. I nearly stepped on Dizzy the Dino."

"Not oatmeal again," Joey said dramatically. "Can't we get some doughnuts?"

"Maybe later," Scott said, remembering how empty the cupboards were. He absolutely had to get to the grocery store today, or they'd be living on peanut butter sandwiches.

The market wasn't the only place he had to go. He'd just finished a job on Ridge Road. Now he had to get going on the café. He'd promised the committee an estimate in a week, and that meant he had to do the calculations this weekend. He planned to give them a rock-bottom price, not that he had any competition in the area, but he wanted to do what he could to help the town survive.

"What are we going to do, Daddy?" Joey asked as he energetically shook the last serving out of a box of dry cereal.

"Let me give it some thought," Scott said as he measured out a scoop of coffee.

"We could go to Uncle Cory and Aunt Doreen's farm."

"Sorry. It's too far for today."

Scott loved his older sister, but he wasn't up to her incessant questioning about his dating life or lack thereof. He didn't know why she was so gung ho to see him married again. Right now he didn't have time for anything but Joey and his job.

"Maybe the zoo," Joey said hopefully.

"Sorry, partner. We're not going to drive all the way to Des Moines."

He had to give Joey the bad news that they were going to the big builders' supply store. It wasn't his son's favorite place, but at least he wouldn't have to have a sitter again this weekend. Scott had promised that he wouldn't. He put bread in the toaster and milk on the table, then watched while Joey poured his own. Most likely he would spill some, but his son loved to be independent.

"Remember when we went to Apple Grove and looked at that old restaurant?" Scott said.

"Yeah, I liked Lori."

Scott was surprised that she'd made an impression on Joey. Unfortunately, it wouldn't do for either of them to get too interested in her. She'd left Apple Grove once, and no doubt she'd do it again as soon as she could.

"She's going to cook there for a little while when I get it fixed up."

"I didn't like it. It was scary."

"It's old and dirty, but I'm going to make it nice again." Scott patted his son's uncombed hair. "It just needs fixing up, and you know that's what I do. I thought you could be my helper today."

"How?" Joey liked specifics.

"What I need to do is a little measuring, and then I have to make a trip to Bensen's."

"That will take forever," Joey wailed.

Joey had trailed after his father too many times in the home improvement superstore. It wasn't his idea of fun by any means.

"I've been thinking," Scott said. "I have a bag of wood scraps in the storage shed. Maybe it's time to get you a hammer and some nails of your own so you can make something."

It was a bribe, but Scott was glad he'd thought of it. Joey didn't have friends his age in the trailer park, and there wasn't much for him to do when he wasn't at day care.

Joey's enthusiasm proved it was a good idea.

"Eat up while I get ready to go. We won't have to spend much time at the café. We'll leave after I have my coffee," Scott told him.

They weren't going to day care. Joey could wear his shirt backward if he wanted to.

It took longer to get going than Scott had hoped. Joey had to fill his backpack with the usual odds and ends, including Dizzy the Dino, who, his son insisted, liked to ride in the truck. Scott ate his toast, then took a few minutes to clean up the kitchen area and flip his bed back into a couch. They weren't likely to have visitors, but he didn't want Joey to grow up thinking it was all right to be messy.

By the time they got to Apple Grove, it was after nine o'clock. Scott parked in front of the café and helped Joey out of his car seat, then took out the key Bess Raymond had given him. With his son at his heels, he went to the front door. It was unlocked. He stuck his head inside and called out loudly, not wanting to startle whoever was there.

"Anybody here?"

There was no answer, so he stepped inside, keeping Joey behind him. It was unlikely, but some transient might have broken in to spend the night.

"Hello! Anybody here?" he called again.

"Oh, I wasn't expecting anybody. Hello! Hi, Joey! What do you have there?" Lori stepped through the swinging doors from the kitchen.

"His name's Dizzy," Joey said, holding the plastic dinosaur up for her inspection.

"Hope I didn't startle you," Scott said. She was like a burst of sunshine in the dingy café.

She shook her head. "No, so many people have an interest in this place that I expect drop-ins. Well, Joey, are you Dad's helper this morning?"

"I'm going to get my own hammer," Joey said excitedly.

"Wonderful! Then you can build things like your daddy," Lori replied.

Scott was pleased that she showered so much attention on Joey. He was reminded of how kind she was, always concerned about other people. Even though they'd never dated, he'd always admired that about her.

She smiled at him, and he grinned back to show her how much he appreciated the attention she was giving Joey.

Did she know about Mandy's death? He knew how gossip circulated in small towns, but possibly she didn't know yet. He wasn't sure how to bring up the subject, and the last thing he wanted was more sympathy. He'd heard enough platitudes to last him a lifetime. He'd finally figured out that saying conventional things helped people deal with a loss, but he much preferred to get past his wife's tragic end.

Had he been straight with Joey when he'd told him his mother had gone to heaven? Or had it been just another platitude? The important thing was that his son was comforted by the idea. He didn't need to know how much Scott was struggling with his own beliefs.

A year ago he'd made the decision to start Joey in Sunday school. He wasn't sure why, but it just felt right to include his son in the life of the church, even though he didn't feel moved to participate himself. Some day Joey would have to decide for himself what his beliefs were. Scott didn't want it on his conscience that he'd failed to expose him to Christian teachings.

Joey chatted with Lori as though he'd known her for ages. He didn't usually take to strangers that quickly.

Taking out the notepad that held all his measurements and specifications, Scott studied the pages. He needed to check a few more things, then wait for the exterminator to give him a copy of his inspection report. It would make a big difference in Scott's estimate if he had to shore up the building the way he had the pharmacy.

"Do you need any help?" Lori asked.

"Thanks, no. I just have a few things to check," Scott said. "What brings you here this morning?"

"Don't laugh, but I was planning the menu."

"It will be a while before you can do any cooking here," he said, laughing.

"Yes, I know, but I was trying to remember what Amos Conklin had on his menu. I want to capture the ambiance of the old café, but with healthier food."

"I liked his pizza. It was great, but oil would run down your arm when you ate it. Great hamburgers, too, about half fat."

"I remember his mashed potatoes. He served them with a big scoop of gravy and a huge pat of real butter. It's hard to make things taste that good and still be heart-healthy."

"I guess most people don't want that kind of food anymore," he said, "but it's a treat once in a while. I love eggs fried in real butter, with hash browns on the side."

"As soon as the café is up and running, I'll fix you a breakfast special that will make your mouth water."

"I'll hold you to it," he said with a grin. "While I have you here, maybe you can give me some idea what type of floor covering you want. I'll be putting in new wall-board, too. It can be wood panels, or I can paint or paper it, whichever you like."

"I'm afraid I'll have to meet with the committee on stuff like that. What do you suggest?"

"I'm not a decorator, but I am on my way to Bensen's to get some quotes. Why don't you come along? Joey and I would love your company. While you're there, you can pick up some tile and wall covering samples to show the committee."

Joey didn't give her a chance to say no, urging her to come with four-year-old fervor.

"You can help me pick out my hammer," he said excitedly.

"If you have something else to do, I can grab a handful of samples for you," Scott said. "I have to warn you, Joey and I plan to stop on the way home at a fast-food place with a play area. You know, slides and a pit full of balls, stuff like that. I'm afraid he'll want to stay awhile." Scott was also afraid she could read in his expression how much he hoped she'd say yes.

"Come with us," Joey said enthusiastically.

Lori tucked a lock of her chestnut hair behind her ear, a gesture that meant she was trying to make up her mind. Scott was surprised that he remembered that little habit of hers.

"I'd love to come with you," she finally said.

Scott was pleasantly surprised and realized he'd been holding his breath, waiting for an answer. What did he think he was doing? He wanted to spend time with her, but asking her to go to a building supply store was about as far from a date as anyone could get.

"Great. Joey will love having you."

"My cell phone doesn't get good reception in here— maybe the tin ceiling or something. Aunt Bess wanted me to go shopping, so I'd better tell her to go ahead without me."

When she went outside, Scott took out his notepad. He relied on it to keep track of the specs for the job. While he worked, Joey occupied himself by tracing his name on the dusty tabletops, a skill he'd just mastered.

His whole mood had brightened. It would be good to have another adult join the two of them, especially since it was Lori.

Lori was older and wiser now, but she still felt a disturbing warmth in Scott's presence. Was it only a remnant of the huge crush she'd once had? She felt drawn to him, but he had a family, a wife and an adorable son.

Lori made a quick call to Bess, letting her know she wouldn't be going shopping with her and the reason why. Of course, her aunt thought it was a splendid idea, although Lori was a little puzzled by her aunt's enthusiasm.

Lori didn't know Scott as a man, and she couldn't help wondering how much he'd changed from the boy she'd known. At any rate, he wasn't available. She was worrying about getting to know him better when nothing could come of it. Going to the store with him was a practical decision. She wanted to do everything she could to get the café up and running. At least then she could leave Apple Grove knowing that her aunt's pet project was under control.

She elected to wait outside while he finished whatever he was doing. In truth, the derelict interior of the café filled her with doubts. By the time it was renovated enough to open, it might be long past her deadline to give a firm answer to the job offer to work at the new restaurant in Chicago. In spite of Lori's determination not to stay in Apple Grove beyond the summer, her aunt was counting on her to revitalize the café. How long would it take to do that? Would the committee be able to hire a replacement chef?

Scott didn't keep her waiting long. He came out and locked the door, his hand on Joey's shoulder to steer him toward the truck.

"I hope you don't mind riding in the jump seat. Joey's car seat isn't secure enough back there."

"No, not at all," Lori said.

"Let me get a wipe," Scott said to his son. "Your hands are filthy."

"I can write my name," Joey proudly told Lori.

"That's great! What are you going to make with your new hammer?" she asked.

"Lots of things. Dizzy needs a house."

"Dizzy?"

"His dinosaur," Scott said, retrieving a moistened wipe from the truck and scrubbing his son's hands.

"Yes, dinosaurs really like having a place of their own," Lori said, playing along.

The ride to Bensen's went more quickly than Lori had expected, and as Scott drove down the rural roads, she admired the recently cultivated fields on either side. The corn was newly planted, making the whole countryside seem fresh and promising. She couldn't ride through rural Iowa without thanking the Lord for the bounty all around her.

The trip went fast because Joey never stopped talking. He was obviously excited about what he would build, and she suspected that it was a treat to have his father's full attention. She wanted to ask about his mother but decided it wasn't her place.

"Bensen's isn't Joey's favorite store," Scott said a bit apologetically when they arrived in the busy parking lot in front of the huge store. "He won't ride in a cart anymore, but it's a lot of walking for a kid his age."

"We'll play the find-it game," Lori said, as they got out of the car.

"What's that?" Joey asked.

"You think of something in the store, and we'll see how fast you can find it. Then I'll think of something. Whoever finds things the fastest wins."

"Daddy will win. He knows where everything is." Joey looked crestfallen.

Lori couldn't help smiling. "Daddy can't play. Just you and me. What shall we look for first?"

She was a little surprised when Joey slipped his hand into hers.

"A hammer!" he squealed with delight.

"Good idea," Scott said. "Let's find your hammer first. Then you have to let Lori and me look at other things."

Joey had no trouble leading them to the right aisle to find a hammer. Lori was a little surprised when Scott started lifting full-sized ones to get a feel for what he wanted.

"Here are some kids' tool sets," she pointed out, unable to see Joey using a heavy grown-up hammer.

"Thanks, but I don't believe in giving kids toy tools. They never work well, and it only frustrates them. Don't worry. Joey won't be using it without my supervision."

"Wow, you're going to get a big man's hammer," she said to Joey.

"I'll teach him the safe way to use it," Scott said. "Now we need to find nails. Joey gets a point for finding the hammer. Let's see who can find the nails first."

Scott and Lori soon conceded the game to Joey. The store was one big maze of shelves and aisles, but the four-year-old had an amazing memory for finding his way around it.

"You can probably tell that we come here a lot," Scott said, letting his son hold the heavy hammer while he picked out an assortment of nails to go with it. "Remember when you helped me build a trellis for your aunt's climbing roses?"

"It's lasted all this time," Lori said. "It's so heavy with roses that it can't even be painted anymore. When you build something, it's certainly sturdy."

"I seem to remember that you were a big help, especially when I spilled the nails and you helped me find them all."

"You're being kind. I was the one who knocked them over."

"Were you?" He laughed. "I don't remember that, but I do remember your purple phase. All you wore were purple shirts."

"That was our school color! I remember you wearing a denim jacket with so many metal studs, you clanked when you walked."

"Guilty," he said, laughing. "Funny what we thought was cool when we were kids. Do you still paint your nails that silvery color? Always reminded me of a robot."

She laughed at his teasing. The years seemed to fall away, and they were kids again, covering up their mutual affection with jokes.

Then, they split up for a moment, Joey choosing to go with her while his dad went to the lumber department. She got lost in the plumbing section and was a bit embarrassed to call on the little boy to lead her to the flooring section.

At the end of their trip, she had a stack of samples and absolutely no ideas about how the café should be decorated. Aunt Bess was expecting Scott to miraculously transform the old café into a town meeting place as well as a restaurant. It wasn't going to be a quick or easy process. Revitalizing the building was going to take a lot of hard work and prayers, not to mention a big investment from the committee members.

"Well, that wasn't so bad, was it?" Scott said to his son when they had paid for their purchases and were out in the parking lot.

He gave Lori his hand to help her into the space behind the driver's seat. His palm was rough and calloused, but his touch was gentle, and she had an odd sensation of vertigo. She shook her head to clear it.

"Fasten your seat belt," Joey reminded her.

"That's right," Scott said, nodding at his son. "The truck won't go unless everyone is belted in."

Scott was bareheaded today, his dark blond hair curling in the back, above the collar of his navy blue T-shirt. She could get only a glimpse of his face in the rearview mirror, and his eyes were masked by sunglasses. She could see his hands on the steering wheel, gripping it tightly as he drove with complete concentration. The deserted country road didn't seem to call for so much intensity, but then, he did have his son beside him on the seat. She could read his determination to keep the little boy safe in the rigid set of his shoulders. Joey kept chattering, but Scott answered only in monosyllables.

When they got to the town where Scott had promised

to stop for lunch, Joey literally bounced in his car seat. Lori wondered when she had last felt enthusiasm like his.

Her fervent prayer was that someday she would have a child of her own, someone to love without reservation. Joey reminded her of what she was missing. Maybe it would never happen. Maybe she would be like Aunt Bess, devoted to following the Lord and doing what she could for others. It was a good life, a satisfying life, but still her heart was moved by Joey, by his innocence and his zest for life.

They stopped, and she got out of the truck while Scott was occupied with extracting Joey from his car seat.

Scott smiled at her warmly and nodded at the rather garish fast-food place, with its enclosed play area on one side.

"Joey's favorite restaurant," he said a bit apologetically.

"I've never been here. It will be a new experience," she said enthusiastically.

They were early for lunch, but still the play area was a busy place. As soon as they went through the restaurant's door, Joey made a beeline for the enclosed play area, with a slide, climbing ropes, places to crawl and an enclosure filled with hundreds of red, green and yellow balls.

"I guess we'd better find a table and order some food," Scott said, with a small smile. "Not that Joey has the slightest interest in eating while he's here."

She followed Scott to a green-topped table where he could keep an eye on his son while he played.

"What can I get for you?" he asked.

"I'd love something cold to drink, but I'm really not hungry," she said.

"Yeah, I feel the same way about the food here," he said,

with a knowing grin. "I'll just get some chicken nuggets and fries, which we can all share, if that's okay with you."

"Fine. I'll just sit and watch Joey. He certainly can climb."

"Like a monkey."

If the noise level was any indication, a dozen or more kids were having the time of their lives. Lori was immensely entertained by their antics and almost tempted to jump into the deep layer of rubber balls, which came up to Joey's waist. He was trying to shimmy across them, sending them flying in all directions.

Scott came back with a tray full of chicken nuggets and French fries, with an apple juice for Joey and tall cups of lemonade for them.

"I'll tell him the food is here," he said.

It was obvious that Joey preferred playing to eating, and Scott was an understanding father. He didn't insist that his son come to the table.

"He'll come when he gets hungry," he said, returning alone.

Lori dipped a limp French fry in the ketchup that she had squeezed from a foil packet, but it was only to have something to do. Now that she was sitting alone with Scott, she didn't know what to say. They sat for several minutes without saying anything, but it was a companionable silence. When he did speak, it was only to comment on how much Joey was enjoying himself.

"So how did you like working in Chicago?" he asked finally.

"I liked it, even though the job didn't work out. I have a chance at another if I make up my mind soon enough," she said.

He nodded but didn't ask any more questions, and his reticence discouraged her from satisfying her curiosity about his wife, although she did wonder why he never mentioned Joey's mother.

"You really do look good," he said after he returned from checking on Joey.

It was the last thing she'd expected him to say, and she didn't know how to respond.

"You're not one of those cooks who enjoy their own food too much," he said.

He smiled directly at her, and it was like the sun coming out on a gloomy day. She wanted to say something nice in return, but she was at a loss for words.

"Here he comes. I knew he'd get hungry eventually." Scott stood to let his son slide into the booth beside him.

"That big kid kept hogging the slide," Joey complained. "He sat there and wouldn't let anyone else go down."

"Maybe he'll be gone when you're done eating. You can play a little longer if Lori doesn't mind," Scott told him.

"No, of course not. I was tempted to jump into those balls myself," Lori confessed.

"Big people aren't supposed to," Joey said, with a worried frown.

"I'm not really going to do it," she assured him.

"Lori is very good at resisting temptation," Scott said.

She couldn't help but notice that Scott didn't smile when he said that.

After letting Joey play awhile longer, they headed home. The little boy dozed off on the way back to Apple Grove, but the silence in the truck felt comfortable. She and Scott had grown up in the same town, had gone to the same schools, and had known the same people.

Their shared history made it unnecessary to fill the time with words.

Joey woke up when she got out of the truck.

"Bye, Lori," he said sleepily.

"Have fun making stuff with your new hammer," she said as she turned to walk up to Aunt Bess's house.

Scott thanked her for coming along. She stood and watched as his truck went down the street and disappeared from sight.

Chapter Four

Lori walked to church beside her aunt, drawing in the sweet scent of spring with every breath. It was the first Sunday in May, and she couldn't have imagined a fairer day. The sky was a beautiful blue, and the sun was almost too warm for the white sweater she was wearing with her light pink dress. A light wind teased her silky flared skirt and caressed her cheeks, and she felt truly at home for the first time since arriving back in town.

"Everyone will be so happy to see you," Bess trilled, hustling along in her pointy-toed shoes with one-inch heels.

She was dressed in one of her standard colors, forest green, but she'd softened the effect by wearing a creamy ruffled blouse with her suit. Bess looked lighthearted, which matched Lori's mood perfectly, although she was hard-pressed to understand the rush of happiness the morning had brought.

Certainly she was pleased to be going to Apple Grove Bible Church again. She'd enjoyed services at a Chicago church, but the congregation was so large that she'd felt lost in the crowd. It would be good to see familiar faces, and she was eager to hear a sermon by the new minister, Reverend Bachman.

Not surprisingly, there was a good crowd milling around outside the open church doors; people were enjoying the pleasant weather and exchanging small talk. The sound of the choir's last-minute practice wafted out, a signal that they had a good fifteen minutes before church began.

"I need to talk to one of the Sunday school teachers," her aunt said. "No need for you to come inside yet, but save me a seat somewhere in the middle."

Lori nodded assent as her aunt hurried off, then looked around for familiar faces.

"Lori Raymond!" a voice behind her said.

"Sara! I wondered whether I'd see you this morning."

"You remember Todd, don't you?" the apple-cheeked, red-haired young woman asked, introducing her husband.

"Of course, you were a few years ahead of us in school. It's nice to see you, Todd," Lori said.

"Lori's been in Chicago, working as a chef," Sara told her husband.

"Here for a vacation?" Todd asked, running his finger around the collar of a crisp white shirt.

He was a big man, muscular but not beefy, with a pleasant face and close-cropped blond hair. Lori remembered him as a popular football player, but as rather shy and quiet.

"Not exactly," Lori said as a trio of little girls in pastel dresses and little straw hats raced past her.

"Oops. Looks like Sunday school is letting out," Sara said. "I'd better round up Sunny. Call me again soon."

When Sara and Todd darted around to the rear entrance to collect their daughter, Lori looked for other people she knew. There were familiar faces, but before she could approach anyone, she was surprised to see the last person she would expect to find at church.

"Scott!" she called.

He stopped suddenly when he saw her and grinned broadly.

"Lori."

"I didn't expect to see you here," she told him.

"No, I suppose you didn't," he said, coming two steps closer.

He was wearing his Sunday-best jeans, if there was such a thing, and the cuffs of a pale blue dress shirt were rolled up to his elbows over golden-tan arms. He wasn't wearing a hat, and his hair looked thick and wavy.

"Well, I'm glad to see you." She was surprised by the pleasure she felt.

"I'm picking Joey up from Sunday school," he explained.

"Oh."

"I'm not staying for the service, though."

"Does Joey enjoy Sunday school?"

"He likes to be with kids his own age."

"Well, I'd better go inside," she said. "Say hello to Joey for me."

"Yeah, waiting isn't Joey's strong suit. I'd better go get him."

For a long moment he didn't move away, and she was conscious of his eyes focused on her. Then he was gone, and the sun seemed to go behind a cloud. She moved slowly toward the open church doors, trying not to think about things that could have been different if they'd been more than friends years ago.

When the service began, Lori tried hard to concentrate. She had to admit that the new minister was a gifted preacher, but her mind kept wandering in spite of her good intentions. She shouldn't be thinking about Scott. After all, he had a family of his own now and a life completely separate from hers. A few brief encounters while they planned renovations in the café shouldn't bring back disturbing feelings. What she really needed to do was decide whether to take the new job in Chicago. That way she would know how long she'd be staying in Apple Grove.

Bess chatted with friends after the service, and Lori stood beside her and answered the same questions over and over as different people greeted her. She loved the people in town, but she had a hard time focusing on the conversations that swirled around her when her own life was in limbo. She found it especially hard to say how long she'd stick around. She was relieved when her aunt finally wanted to start walking home.

"Oh, by the way," Bess said in an offhand way, "I've invited company for Sunday dinner. That potato salad you made last night looks too luscious for just the two of us. I hope you don't mind."

"Well, no, of course not."

"I have some hot dogs and buns. We can fire up my grill. I made sure there's enough charcoal."

The last time Lori had eaten anything her aunt had grilled, she'd had to scrape off a quarter inch of charred meat. Bess was a wonderful teacher but a disaster as a cook.

"I'll take care of the grill," Lori quickly offered.

"I was sure I could count on you," her aunt said, with a little giggle. "And don't worry about dessert. I have three kinds of ice cream in the freezer."

"You didn't say who's coming."

"Dottie. You remember her. We've been teaching together since forever. And I invited Scott when I saw him picking Joey up after Sunday school."

Scott had doubts—serious doubts—about going to Bess Raymond's house for Sunday dinner. If she had any ideas about matching him with her niece, she was wasting her time. A lot had happened since high school. He felt hollow inside, and he was not ready to let anyone else get close. His life was much more complicated now than when they'd been kids.

Even if he did want to renew his friendship with Lori, nothing could come of it. She'd be leaving after the café was up and running. He didn't want Joey to become attached to her, only to be devastated when she left.

He was mad at himself for not thinking of an excuse to get out of going to Sunday dinner, but Miss Raymond had a way of getting people to do what she wanted. Going to a meal at her house was the second thing he really didn't want to do that day.

Joey was hyper after Sunday school, and Scott nearly canceled their trip to the cemetery on Ridge Road. But today would have been Mandy's twenty-fifth birthday, and Joey had carefully selected a bouquet of yellow and white flowers for her grave. Scott couldn't give him a new mother, not now and maybe never, but he could keep her memory alive for the son who would never know her.

It was the least he could do for her.

Mandy's marker was one of the flat bronze ones in the new section, but Scott had to drive through the old cemetery to get there.

"Why are there houses here?" Joey asked.

"People built them a long time ago to remember people they cared about."

"Why doesn't Mom have one?"

"People don't do that anymore."

"They don't remember anymore?"

"No, people can live in your heart without you building a mausoleum—that's what they're called."

"What's inside them?" Joey's curiosity wasn't easily satisfied.

"They're mostly empty, I guess." The last thing he wanted was to get into a discussion about caskets and vaults. "Miss Raymond invited us for Sunday dinner. I think she's going to have hot dogs," he said, changing the subject.

"We had those last night."

Joey's lack of enthusiasm mirrored his own, and he wondered if he should cancel. He decided it was too late to come up with a plausible excuse.

He parked the pickup on a narrow dirt road, and they walked the short distance to Mandy's family plot. Her parents had insisted she be laid to rest there, beside her grandmother and great-grandparents. It was their way of taking her back into their family after she'd married so young and started her own.

Now they'd moved away, trying to run away from

their grief by starting over in another state. It meant that Joey hardly knew his maternal grandparents, one more loss in his young life.

Scott handed the bunch of flowers to Joey and stood back while his son carefully put them in a vase embedded in the ground.

"They'll need water," Scott said, trying to sound more cheerful than he felt as he handed a can of water to his son.

As far as he knew, they were the only ones who still came to Mandy's grave site. Was he doing the right thing by trying to make his son feel connected to his mother? Scott knew that she had loved their baby son, and it felt right to remind Joey of that. Maybe the day would come when Joey wouldn't want to come, but for now it still seemed important to him.

That day had come for Scott. He didn't want to keep reliving her death in his mind, and coming here only renewed his regrets. He wished that he'd loved Mandy enough to get beyond the anger and guilt he still felt. Until he did, he couldn't move on.

For his own peace of mind, he had to stop daydreaming about Lori. It didn't help that she was even more beautiful than he remembered. He'd never seen hair that vibrant on anyone else, a deep chestnut brown with reddish tints, which had glowed this morning when he saw her in the bright sunshine. She'd always taken life seriously, but her dark eyes sparkled with liveliness, contradicting her somber side.

He shook his head to chase away her image. Joey was through watering and arranging the flowers, managing to finish with only minimal splashing on his jeans.

"Does Mommy see the flowers from heaven?" he asked in his most serious voice.

"I hope so," Scott said, never sure what to say to his son when he asked hard questions. "We'd better get to Miss Raymond's house. She'll be looking for us."

"You said we'd have mac and cheese for lunch," Joey accused as he hustled back to the truck.

"That was before we were invited to Sunday dinner. We'll have it for supper."

He was thinking of reasons to leave as soon as the meal was over. Sunday dinner with Lori was not a good idea.

Lori rummaged through her aunt's cupboards, finally finding a new jar of peanut butter. If Joey didn't like hot dogs, she could whip him up a peanut butter and jelly sandwich. She fussed with the platter of carrot sticks, celery stuffed with cream cheese, cheese chunks and crackers, adding a few saltines in case the four-year-old didn't like the wheat crackers. She wasn't sure what pre-school kids liked to eat, so it would be fun testing recipes for a cookbook devoted to them. She expected to receive the first bunch of recipes soon.

"That will do nicely," Bess said. "I'm sure we have plenty of food."

Her aunt was right, of course. Lori was doing what she always did when she was nervous: puttering in the kitchen. She didn't say so, but inviting Scott's family for Sunday dinner was not a good idea. She had to work with him on the café renovations, but she'd already decided to spend as little time with him as possible. He was, after all, a married man, an uncomfortably attractive one.

"Oh, get the door, would you please?" her aunt said when the bell rang.

Lori moved slowly to answer the summons. She'd avoided asking Scott about his wife, not expecting to see either of them socially. Scott had not mentioned his wife to Lori and she didn't know what to expect.

She opened the door, curious but also uneasy about meeting Scott's wife. She wanted to like her for his sake.

"Hi, Lori!" Joey said, with a grin.

There were only the two of them, and Joey skirted around her, his attention caught by the bowl of goldfish Bess kept in the living room.

"Look, but don't touch," his father quickly warned.

Lori hesitated, not sure what to say. "I thought—"

"It was nice of your aunt to invite us," Scott said very formally, stepping into the room when she backed up.

"I thought, that is, I was sure the invitation included your wife."

She couldn't read his expression, but his jaw was clenched and his eyes seemed to cloud over.

"I mean, it's none of my business." Lori was mortified that she might have said something wrong.

"My wife is deceased," he said quietly. "She's been gone since Joey was a baby."

"Oh, Scott, I'm sorry. I had no idea."

"There's no reason why you should've known." He sounded like a tired stranger, not the person she'd known years ago.

"Daddy, there are three fish," Joey interrupted excitedly.

"He's learning to count," Scott said, sounding grateful for the intrusion. "Be careful not to knock the bowl over," he warned his son.

"Hello," Bess said, coming into the room. "If you like pets, I have someone you'd like to meet, Joey."

"Is it a dog?" the little boy asked.

"No, guess again," said Bess.

"A cat?" he said, with a little less enthusiasm.

Bess shook her head. "Not even close. You'll just have to come out back with me to meet Petey."

"I wouldn't put it past your aunt to have a pony back there," Scott said, obviously trying to sound enthusiastic.

"No, Petey is a rabbit," Lori told him. "One of her students gave it to her a couple of years ago. It's not a very exciting pet, I'm afraid, but Joey can let it out of the pen. It's bigger than a cat and loves to eat."

She was babbling, conscious that Scott wasn't the least bit interested in the rabbit. How could Bess not have told her about Scott's wife? How could Scott not have told her? She was angry and embarrassed, but mostly she felt absolutely terrible for Scott. He was so young to be a widower.

She went on, aware that she was babbling to cover her discomfort. "Aunt Bess has the grill going. I'll watch the hot dogs, though. Her idea of done is charcoal black. But you probably know her reputation as a cook. You were brave to come here, actually, but I made the potato salad. Maybe Joey won't like it, but I can make a peanut butter sandwich if he would prefer it. Come on out to the backyard. We're eating out there."

"Lori, slow down. It's okay." He had always been able to read her feelings no matter how hard she tried to conceal them.

Her heart went out to him when she heard the weary

tone in his voice, but all she could think to say was, "I really am sorry."

Joey rushed back into the living room, insisting his dad come see the rabbit. Watching them go, she wanted to cry but couldn't let herself.

She heard her aunt come back to the kitchen and hurried to confront her.

"Why didn't you tell me?" she asked in a strangled whisper.

"Tell you what, dear?" Bess took out a large container of lemonade.

"That Scott's wife is dead!"

"You didn't know?"

"No, I didn't know!"

Bess looked stricken, plopping down the lemonade and dropping onto one of the kitchen chairs.

"Oh, dear, it never crossed my mind that you might not know. I mean, you went with him to get samples. You were with him most of the day. Sweetie, everyone in town knows. I never even thought that you might not—please, don't be angry with me."

"I'm not angry," Lori said sadly. "I'm only sorry for Scott and Joey."

She hugged her aunt. She was starting toward the backyard when a shrill cry sent them both running out of the house.

Chapter Five

The crisis was well in hand when they walked down the steps to Bess's large, well-tended backyard. Petey the rabbit had mustered an unusual amount of energy and had hopped toward the neighbor's yard while Joey was trying to pet him. Scott had quickly caught him and returned him to the spot where Joey had been playing with him.

Dottie, who'd gone directly to the backyard instead of coming to her old friend's front door, was soothing Joey, assuring him that he could feed Petey some lettuce. She came over and hugged Lori, beaming and giving her a big wink.

Like her aunt, Dottie was a leader in the community, a devoted church member and a teacher, as well as one of the people who'd invested in the café. But unlike Bess, she was rail thin and inclined to be outspoken. When she got an idea in her head, she was as unstoppable as a freight train.

What was with the wink? It didn't take Lori long to figure it out.

"I'm so happy to be here with you young people," Dottie said. "Hasn't Lori bloomed into a lovely young woman, Scott?"

"Yes, she has," Scott agreed.

"Apple Grove is so fortunate to have Scott," Dottie observed. "I don't know who would renovate the café if he didn't live here. We've heard wonderful things about his work."

Bess had the grace to look embarrassed by her friend's high-handed attempt at matchmaking, but Lori didn't doubt that she supported the effort wholeheartedly.

Lori gave the hot dogs on the grill far more attention than they needed. Her heart was breaking for Joey, who was without a mother to love and cherish him, and she was having a hard time holding back tears for Scott. How terrible for him to find someone to love, then lose her so soon.

She'd known there was something different about Scott. Now she realized that it was loneliness and sorrow. He seemed to be going through the motions of living, but his zest for life wasn't there anymore. More than ever, she wished that he could turn to the Lord for strength and consolation.

"He's running away!" Joey shrieked. "Petey is running away again!"

"Don't worry, sweetie," Bess assured him, with a kindly laugh. "He never goes far."

Scott ran after the rabbit and scooped him up, putting him down in front of his son again.

"There. He just needed a little exercise. You can pet him one more time. Then he needs to go back in his pen so you can wash your hands for dinner."

"Dad, he wants to play with me," Joey said, stroking the big, fluffy rabbit between his ears.

"Maybe after dinner," Scott said, returning the rabbit to the wire-fronted pen.

"He's an old bunny. He needs a little rest," Bess said. "What kind of ice cream do you like, Joey? I have vanilla, chocolate and butter pecan."

"Chocolate. I like chocolate," Joey said.

"Good. We'll have ice cream cones for dessert. Now run along with your daddy and get washed up," Bess told him. "Dottie will help Lori and me put the food on the picnic table."

Lori busied herself by slicing halfway through the hot dogs and adding strips of cheddar, then leaving them on the grill just long enough for the cheese to get bubbly. Then she put the hot dogs into buns that had been heating on one end of the grill, in a big foil packet.

She had found canned baked beans in her aunt's pantry and had spiced them up with thinly sliced onion, mustard, brown sugar and her own blend of spices. It wasn't gourmet cooking, but it made the beans a little more appealing after they were heated in the oven. She'd used her mother's recipe for potato salad, mainly because her aunt was especially fond of it. It had sat overnight to let the ingredients blend: new potatoes, celery, onions, eggs and a mayo mix. Just to be sure there was something that Joey might like, she'd opened a can of applesauce and added some cinnamon.

When they were all seated at the table, Bess said grace, thanking the Lord for the bounty before them and for good friends with whom to share it.

"Can I play with Petey after I eat?" Joey asked, more interested in the rabbit than the food.

"He may be taking a nap," Bess said, tactfully leaving the decision to Scott.

"We'll see," his father said. "I thought you wanted to go to the park."

Joey nodded. "After I play with Petey. Can I get a rabbit of my own?"

"Not right now. He'd be too lonesome with neither of us home all day," Scott pointed out.

"Maybe he could go to day care with me."

"Mrs. Drummond would love that," Scott said, with a grin that softened the intensity in his eyes.

He doesn't want to be here, Lori realized. It's as awkward for him as it is for me, knowing that Bess wants to get us together. Her aunt could be scatter-brained, but how could she have neglected to mention anything about Scott's wife?

Lori would have to be firm with her. She'd agreed to help with the café, but in return, Bess would have to promise not to throw her in Scott's path. Her aunt had to accept that Lori was staying only as long as it took to get another job. She'd enjoyed living in a large metro-politan area, meeting new people all the time and attend-ing Chicago Cubs baseball games whenever possible. A big city had a lot to offer, even if the cost of living forced her to watch her money closely.

She knew she'd have to make a decision about the job offer in Chicago soon, in fairness to herself and her aunt. No doubt the staff at the new restaurant could help her find a roommate and affordable housing.

Why shouldn't she take the job? she asked herself.

She was fond of Apple Grove and the people there, but she'd grown beyond the small town, hadn't she?

After a bit of encouragement, Joey started eating, preferring his hot dog cut up in pieces with the cheese scraped away. She should have thought of leaving one plain, but she hadn't cooked for kids since her babysitting days.

"I have to tell you, Scott, the committee was pleased with your bid," Dottie said, taking a tiny bite of potato salad. "An hourly wage plus materials is more than fair. You can get started on the work as soon as possible. Can you meet with us some evening soon—you, too, Lori— and go over the specifics, the decor and such?"

"I'm sure I can," Scott agreed.

Bess passed the bowl of potato salad and the plate of hot dogs, then nudged the dish of beans closer to Scott, apparently content to let her friend speak for the committee.

"When can you get started on the work?" Dottie asked.

Scott thought for a moment. "I'll start tearing things out tomorrow, right after I place an order for materials. Some may have to be shipped here from Des Moines."

"I'm sure you'll get moving on it as quickly as you can," Bess said. "Now, Joey, would you like a little more applesauce?"

Lori watched the others eat, forcing herself to finish the tiny portions on her plate. Scott divided his attention between his son and the two older women, not looking in Lori's direction. She preferred it that way. What more could she say, except to repeat how sorry she was about his wife?

She volunteered herself to fix the ice cream cones, although only Bess and Joey wanted one. At least she could escape to the kitchen, where she wouldn't have to struggle to make conversation. She scooped chocolate ice cream for Joey and butter pecan for her aunt, then grabbed a dish towel to protect the little boy's clothes from stains.

As soon as Joey began his cone, she realized that she'd given him more than he could handle. Scott pushed the ice cream farther into the cone to cut down on dripping and cautioned his son to forget about the rabbit and to eat the cone right away. After a while, Joey gave up on the now-soggy cone, and his father took him inside again to wash up.

"Well, this was a pleasant dinner," Bess said. "It's so nice that it's warm enough for a picnic."

Lori had a lot to say to her aunt, but now wasn't the time. She busied herself with clearing the table, waiting to carry things inside until Scott came back outside so she wasn't in the house when he was.

"Can I help you clean up?" he asked when he returned.

"I wouldn't hear of it," Bess said. "You young folks go over to the park. I'm not much of a cook, but I'm good at cleaning up. I'm sure Dottie will help me."

"I'll help you, too," Lori quickly insisted.

"No, days like this are a gift. You have a nice walk over to the park. It will do you good to get some fresh Iowa air," Bess said.

Lori hadn't even thought of going with Scott and his son, but Joey latched on to the idea.

"Come with us, Lori. Please? You can watch me on the monkey bars. I'm getting good at them. 'Course, Daddy has to help. He broke his arm once, so he wants me to be careful."

Lori was about to make an excuse not to go, but Scott didn't give her a chance.

"Joey will be disappointed if you don't come."

Joey might be, but what about his father? What could she possibly say to him? They'd been close friends once, but sympathy wasn't a good basis for a renewed friendship. She felt terrible about the loss of his wife, but what a klutz she'd been! Why hadn't she asked about his wife sooner? It was the natural thing to do after she met his son.

Why hadn't she asked who he'd married? If she'd known her? Was his wife from Apple Grove?

Maybe she hadn't wanted to know. Scott had once been so important to her that she'd shied away from knowing about his life now. She wanted him to be the boy she'd adored, not a stranger with a wife and son.

She felt like an absolute fool. What could she possibly say to him to make up for it?

No, she definitely wasn't going to the park!

She opened her mouth to refuse, determined to resist, no matter what Bess or Joey or Scott said.

"I think we have a few things to straighten out," Scott said in a soft voice, which didn't carry over to the grill, where Bess was gathering up the fork and padded glove.

Lori shrugged. "Maybe another time."

"Please come now," Scott insisted. "It's only a couple of blocks. I won't keep you long if you don't want to stay."

What could they possibly have to say to each other? She didn't know, but something in Scott's voice made it impossible to refuse. She reluctantly agreed.

Scott hoisted his son onto his shoulders for the walk to the park. In spite of all her misgivings about being anywhere near him, she realized that she couldn't just walk away from the man. They would have to work together on plans for the café, much as she would like to get out of it and get on with her life. Whatever he had to say to her, maybe it was better to get it over with.

Scott was angry at himself for creating a situation that made Lori uncomfortable. He should have told her about Mandy right away. He'd had plenty of chances when she went to Bensen's with him.

Joey was getting heavy to carry on his shoulders. The little rascal kept bouncing up and down, playing pony and forcing Scott to keep a firm hold on his legs so he wouldn't fall off. Lori was walking a step behind them, so he couldn't see her. They ran out of sidewalk at the end of the street, and he started across the town's baseball field to the town park, where there was play equipment. He wished Mrs. Drummond would take the kids outside more, but he knew that she didn't take suggestions well. He couldn't risk losing Joey's place in her day care. No other good alternative existed in town at the moment, although he'd heard rumors that a day care might start up in the church basement.

It was a nice enough park for the size of the town. The monkey bars, Joey's favorite, were the old-fashioned kind made of metal pipes. Fortunately, the row of overhead bars wasn't very high, and the ground below it had a thick covering of wood chips. Still, Scott liked to stand under the monkey bars while his son worked his way to the other side. Joey was still a little shaky, especially when he got to the end and had to get his feet onto the ladder to get down.

"Watch me, Lori," Joey yelled, twisting his head to be sure he had an audience.

"You're doing great," she said when he reached the end of the bars.

Scott knew from experience that his son would want to go back and forth a dozen times before he moved on to the other play equipment. Today this was good. He wanted to talk to Lori, but he didn't know where to begin.

At last Joey's arms got tired, and he excitedly asked Lori to push him on one of the big swings.

"Not too high," Scott cautioned when she agreed, then quickly realized that he wasn't giving her credit for any common sense.

"How about this one?" Lori asked, going over to a wooden seat with a safety bar, which hung beside the others.

"That's a baby swing," Joey said a bit indignantly, trying to plop himself down on the lowest seat in the row.

Lori gave him a boost, and they both laughed with pleasure when she gave him a shove to get him started.

Scott was more than content to watch. He'd forgotten how graceful Lori was and how kind she could be. She made a show of pushing Joey way up in the sky, but she made sure that his perch was secure and he didn't go too high.

Her arms had to be tired, but she cheerfully kept pushing until Joey finally was ready to stop swinging.

He slipped off the seat and looked around for the next thing he wanted to try. Scott already knew that he'd want to slide, but first he wanted a few minutes of Lori's attention.

He turned to his son. "Joey, how about playing in the sandbox for a while? Someone left a dirt truck there."

"Dad, I want to slide."

"In a little while," Scott promised.

Joey was easily persuaded to play with the green-and-yellow plastic dump truck that had been abandoned in the sandbox. Scott led Lori to one of the picnic tables far enough away to let them talk, but close enough to keep his eye on his son.

"I'm never around children," she said a little breathlessly. "Joey certainly has a lot of energy."

"Yeah, and he doesn't take naps anymore. By seven tonight he'll be exhausted. Some days I can hardly wait until it's his bedtime."

"I imagine he would wear anyone out."

She kept her eyes on his son, making it harder for Scott to begin the conversation he thought they should have.

"I'm going to stop wearing my wedding ring," he said, barely speaking above a whisper. "It's time. I can see why you were misled."

"Not because…"

"Wait. Let me finish."

She turned to look at him and nodded assent.

"I should have told you about Mandy. There was no reason not to."

"Why didn't you?"

He shook his head. "I don't know. It's hard to talk about her, especially when Joey is listening. But I can see how awkward it was for you, not knowing."

"That doesn't matter," she said. "I'm only sorry you lost someone you loved."

"I don't want sympathy." He blurted out the words,

then regretted them. "I mean, it was more than three years ago. Joey and I have moved on."

"I understand."

He wondered if she possibly could. It was tempting to pour out all his feelings. Lori was the best listener he'd ever known, but sometimes words weren't enough. Anyway, the last thing he wanted was pity from her.

She didn't ask him any more questions. Her silence was a gift, and he appreciated it.

"Lori! Come see the mountain I've made!"

Joey yelled loud enough to be heard in the next county, and Scott followed Lori to the edge of the sandbox. He could see that his son was a virtual sandman. It would take a lot scrubbing to get the sand out of his scalp. In fact, he'd better strip him down outside if he didn't want grit from one end of the trailer to the other. He should've been watching more closely.

"Wow," Lori said. "You are some digger."

"Can I take the truck home, Daddy?"

"Better leave it here. The person who lost it might come back for it," Scott told him.

A lost truck could be retrieved, but the past couldn't be relived. He wasn't sorry that he'd seen Lori again, but they didn't have anyplace to go from here.

Scott brushed off his son and agreed to three turns down the slide. Not surprisingly, Lori said goodbye to them and started walking home alone.

He watched her move across the baseball field and disappear from sight. Every instinct he had urged him to go after her, but even if he caught up, what then? He had nothing to offer her. He'd loved her once, or he thought he had, but that was a long time ago.

* * *

Lori felt her emotions rising to the surface. Scott's single status shouldn't matter to her, but her heart reached out to him. There must be something she could say to comfort him, but she was afraid that anything she said would only open old wounds. She hated feeling so helpless, especially with an old and once dear friend.

Her first thought was to run home and go to her bedroom where she could think things through in private, but she forced herself to walk at a slow, measured pace, her head held high and her eyes straight ahead.

No way would she turn around to look, but she felt sure that Scott was watching her leave.

What had happened back there? Scott had apologized for not telling her about his wife, but she still felt uncomfortable about not asking. He had taken the blame for his silence, but why had he mentioned being ready to take off his wedding ring? Had he been using the ring as a shield against possible relationships? If so, why had he told her he was ready to stop wearing it?

The only thing she knew for sure was that she should leave Apple Grove for good as soon as possible. However much Scott might have changed, there was still a deep chasm between them. If the tragedy of losing his wife hadn't brought him closer to the Lord, nothing she could say or do would sway him. They had nothing in common except a long-ago friendship that had never blossomed into a relationship.

The best thing for her to do was to stay as far away from him as possible. She couldn't break her promise to her aunt, but she had to make her understand the situation. Bess had to be told not to set up any meetings or meals or anything else that involved both her niece and Scott. Lori had to squelch the matchmaking, and the best way to do that was to accept the Chicago job.

Lori got back to the house full of resolve, but her aunt was nowhere to be seen. The house was empty, and dishes from the picnic dinner were still unwashed beside the kitchen sink.

Had Bess hurried off to yet another meeting with the café committee members, or was she just eager to tell her friends about the Sunday dinner? Apple Grove didn't need the Internet. Everyone knew everything that went on with alarming speed, which made it even more strange that Lori hadn't heard a word about Scott's wife's death before today.

Maybe it was a sign that she really didn't belong there anymore.

Chapter Six

Cleaning ovens was Lori's least favorite job, but she arrived at the café early Monday morning determined to get started on the huge gas range. The committee had decided that they had to keep it for now. The renovations were going to be much more expensive than they'd originally anticipated, even with Scott keeping costs to a minimum. There just wasn't enough money in their budget to buy a new range.

Scott wasn't there yet. She'd gotten up early, eager to finish cleaning the range without being in his way. Since he had to take Joey to day care, she might have several hours to work alone.

Last night she'd prayed hard and long, beseeching God to have compassion on Scott and his motherless son. She didn't believe that he was ready to get on with his life, no matter what he said about taking off his wedding ring. If only he would reach out to the Lord, he would find comfort and renewed purpose in his life.

Putting on a mask, she sprayed the interiors of the two

deep ovens with cleaner. It had to work for at least thirty minutes before she could begin wiping away the loosened grime, so she turned her attention to another task.

Money for renovations was going to be tight, and several committee members had wondered if anything in the café could be sold to help out. Bess had volunteered to have her niece search the place for items to send to an auction.

Lori knew there was a virtual treasure trove of old containers and such in the cellar, things that might tempt collectors to pay a good price. She'd brought a few empty boxes from home to set aside items with potential.

The kitchen had plenty of drawers and cupboards, given that it was a closed-in, cramped space. When Scott tore out one wall to build a pass-through counter, a row of storage would have to go, but it would create more space to move around.

She opened the first drawer, but it was empty except for the stained paper lining. The next one wasn't any more promising, but she did spot a pretzel tucked into a back corner. She reached for it, glad that there were no signs that mice had been nibbling on it.

Much to her surprise, the pretzel was cold and hard, a realistic metal copy, right down to dots representing salt. She was puzzling over its use when she heard someone at the front door.

"Hello. You in here, Lori?"

Scott must have had the same idea about getting to work early. She ignored the little twinge of excitement she felt at the sound of his voice and pushed open one of the swinging doors.

"Good morning," he said. "You're here early."

"Cleaning the range. I wanted to get it over with."

He put down his tool chest and pushed back the old straw hat. His eyes were darkly shadowed, and her heart went out to him, even though she knew he might resent it. It must be terribly difficult to be a good father and still work hard at a job.

"Yeah, I thought they'd get rid of that white elephant, but taking out the window and replacing the glass to get it out was too expensive. Has the gas been turned on yet?"

"No, not yet."

"Well, be sure someone from the gas company inspects it before you try to light the stove," he said, smiling to show that it was only a friendly warning.

"I will. Well, I'll let you get to work."

"Will you be here long? I'll be taking down the old wallboard, and it's going to get pretty dusty."

"I have a mask. I wouldn't stick my head in an oven without one."

"Yes, you always did have good sense. What's that thing in your hand?" he asked.

"A metal pretzel I found in one of the drawers. The committee wants me to look for things they can auction off."

He walked over and took it from her, returning it after a quick glance.

"It's a soda bottle opener, a really old cast-iron one. I know a guy who collects them. He'd pay good money for an unusual one like this."

"Well, that's good to know. Thanks. I'll let you get to work now."

She went back to the kitchen and checked her watch. She couldn't leave until the oven cleaner had done its work and was removed from the ovens. On the other side of the swinging doors, Scott was starting the day's demolition. She was tempted to watch him work, but she had something to tell him. It wouldn't feel right giving him her big news while he was banging his hammer and pulling off old wallboard.

The cupboards were empty except for an old strainer with a hole in it. Lori put it in a box with the bottle opener, but she suspected it would go into the trash after Bess saw it.

If there was a worse kitchen job than oven cleaning, she didn't know what it was. While she waited to wipe down the ovens, she put on rubber gloves that came up to her elbows to clean the surface of the stove.

She'd made her decision and called her future employer to accept the job at an upscale restaurant in suburban Chicago. He wouldn't need her until after Labor Day, which gave her enough time to help open the café, if the renovations went as fast as everyone hoped they would. The restaurant would specialize in continental cuisine and give her a chance to show what she was capable of doing. She wouldn't be relegated to washing vegetables and running errands for the head chef, as she had in her old job.

Aunt Bess had been a good sport when Lori had told her, although she couldn't completely mask her disappointment.

A half hour passed, and Lori armed herself with vinegar, water and a bag of her aunt's old rags to tackle the ovens. The racket from Scott's demolition rang in her ears, but she didn't need the noise to remind her that he was there. It meant a lot to her that they'd reaffirmed their friendship. She'd had other boyfriends since high school, but no one had stirred her innermost feelings quite the way he had. Her decision to accept the Chicago job was the right one—she couldn't be her aunt's guest indefinitely—but her one regret was that Scott would be out of her life forever.

Most of the grime and burnt-on grunge in the ovens came off easily, but one of the racks wouldn't come clean. It was lying on newspaper on the counter, defying her efforts to restore it. She tried steel wool, but something black and rubbery was practically fused to the metal.

The easy solution was to put the rack back in the oven and forget it, but she'd promised to put the kitchen in order. That meant everything had to be sparkling clean when she turned it over to whoever would be the permanent cook.

"Everything all right in here?" Scott asked, sticking his head into the kitchen after a few minutes of silence.

"I've met my match trying to get this thing clean," she said, "but I'm nothing if not stubborn."

He laughed. "Come see what I've done here. This building is even older than I thought."

He held one of the swinging doors open while she stepped out into the partially demolished room.

He pointed. "Look. I moved the counter and found a whole cache of old coins. Here's an Indian Head penny. Don't know that I've ever seen one before."

"I wonder how they got there."

"They must have slipped through a crack between the base and the outer paneling. It's amazing what gets lost in old buildings."

"I don't think anyone would mind if you put them in Joey's piggy bank."

"I couldn't do that," he gently protested. "Look. This dime is real silver. Maybe there are some coins here that will help out with refurnishing the place."

"You're right, but I bet some contractors wouldn't be as honest as you are," she said.

"Maybe not, but I sleep well nights." He smiled warmly and picked up a thermos sitting by his tool chest. "Join me in a coffee break?"

"I'm ready for a break, but I'll pass on the coffee."

"Probably not gourmet enough for you," he teased. "I'm curious what you'll be cooking up in the café."

"Oh, Rock Cornish hens with wild rice stuffing, moussaka, lobster thermidor. You know, a few of my favorites."

He raised one eyebrow in mock skepticism.

"I'm kidding, Scott." Lori smiled, then said, "You know, I've accepted a job in Chicago starting after Labor Day."

"Congratulations."

"Thank you."

Did she expect him to be disappointed? Of course not! So why did she feel so let down? It was the right decision. She'd worked for years for an opportunity like this.

"Well, guess I'd better get back to work," he said. "I really do hope that things work out for you."

She thanked him again and went back to her chores in the kitchen.

Her eyes were tearing up, and she blamed it on the strong chemicals she was using. She had to give the oven rack yet another coat of cleaner, refusing to admit it couldn't be restored. That meant waiting for the cleaner to work again. She took off her rubber gloves and mask, prepared to do whatever had to be done to make the ovens totally clean.

She could go out to the alley behind the café for some fresh air, but half an hour of waiting, with nothing to do, seemed terribly tedious. Instead, she built up her resolve to finish the hunt for salable odds and ends. There was nowhere else to look in the kitchen, but she knew the cellar had potential.

The cellar was a dank, dark hole and the last place she wanted to explore. Still, someone had to do it, and she'd taken on the responsibility. She tried to bolster her courage.

What was the worst that could happen down there? A mouse could run over her foot, but the poor little things were a lot more scared of her than she was of them.

The dark didn't scare her, so she had no logical reason to be afraid of going down there.

She grabbed one of the empty boxes, opened the old wooden door and flicked the switch to light the single dim bulb at the bottom of the steps. The railing was on the left, and she remembered how wobbly it was. She took hold of it, anyway, and wasn't pleased to feel it jiggle under her hand.

The safest way to go down was to take it one step at a time, not moving to the next step until both feet were securely planted. It occurred to her that a flashlight would be a big help, but she could just strip the shelves and put things in boxes to be examined later in the light upstairs.

"Now why is it that you hate cellars?" she asked herself aloud.

The smell was certainly part of the reason. The odor

that wafted up to her was unmistakably that of an un-ventilated cellar, musty, mousy and unpleasant.

"You're being a sissy," she reprimanded herself, not liking the way her voice echoed off the old walls.

A lot of restaurants had cellar storage rooms. It was part of a chef's job to know the inventory and fetch things when needed, although as cellars went, this one was an unsavory pit.

She grew impatient with her slow descent and started moving down the normal way, wondering how many trips it would take to clear all the shelves. With only two steps to go, she let go of the shaky railing—and plunged down to the rough concrete floor.

Scott paused for a moment to take a few sips of coffee from the big insulated cup he brought with him on the job. Removing the old wallboard was messy work, and he'd be glad when this part was done. The hot liquid lubricated his throat, always dry when he had to wear the mask.

Lori had decided to go back to Chicago. He couldn't blame her. Once upon a time he'd badly wanted to leave Apple Grove and see more of the world. He'd thought of joining the military or maybe just bumming his way across the country, doing odd jobs while he figured out what he wanted to do with his life. Things hadn't worked out that way for him, and now it was too late. Joey had changed everything, and he wouldn't trade his son's happiness for anything.

Much as he applauded Lori's spunk in leaving not once, but twice, he hated to see her go. During the short while she'd been here, he'd shaken off some of the emptiness that he'd felt since Mandy's death. If she'd lived, they would have separated. They'd married too young and too quickly, neither realizing that their infatuation wasn't enough to build a life together.

He was about to resume work when he heard something, a muffled shriek that could only be coming from the rear of the building. He ran toward the kitchen, jumping over debris from the walls.

"Lori, are you okay?"

There was no answer, and she wasn't in the kitchen. The door to the alley was shut, but the cellar door was ajar. He took one look and sprinted down the cellar stairs two at a time.

Lori was just pulling herself into a sitting position.

"Watch out for the step!" she cried out.

Her warning wasn't necessary. He could see where the next-to-last step had collapsed.

"Are you hurt?" he asked.

He jumped down and knelt beside her.

She made a muffled little sound and held out her hands. Even in the dim light, he could see how badly she'd scraped them when she landed on the floor.

"The step just gave way," she said, shivering from the shock of her fall.

"Where does it hurt?"

"Everywhere—I don't know—my hands, my knees."

He could see that one leg of her jeans was shredded and reddened with blood.

"I don't think anything's broken," she said with a fainthearted attempt at a smile. "I feel so stupid!"

"I should have warned you not to come down here until I repaired the stairs."

"I should've figured that out for myself." She looked at her hands, holding them with the fingers curled. Her palms were bloody.

"Let's get you upstairs. Put your arms around my neck, and I'll carry you."

"No, I can walk." She tried to pull herself up, then gasped when she reached out with her injured hands to grasp an unbroken step for leverage.

He shook his head at her stubbornness, then smiled in spite of her predicament. This was the old Lori, determined to do things her way.

"I'm a volunteer fireman," he said.

"Good for you." She was twisting around, trying to get leverage with her elbows.

"That means I'm trained to carry people over my shoulder in an emergency."

"This isn't an emergency. Just give me a little boost."

He scooped her up in his arms, giving her no choice but to cling to his neck.

She was petite by anyone's standards, but carrying a hundred or so pounds up the rickety stairs was no snap. He had to skip the broken step carefully and test every board before he could risk putting all their weight on it.

"Scott, I can walk!"

He didn't have the breath to argue. His body was conditioned for hard work, but he rarely had time to run or lift weights anymore. By the time he reached the top of the stairs, he was more than willing to let her slide from his arms.

"Well, thank you, but I can walk."

She hobbled over to the nearest counter and leaned heavily against it.

He pulled off his work gloves and followed her, reaching out to take one of her hands as gently as he could. He was no medic, but the grit embedded in her palms couldn't be good.

"I'd better wash my hands," she said. "Are there any chairs out there? I feel a little dizzy."

"Here." He lifted her up onto the counter and stood there to make sure she didn't pass out and fall.

"I have to finish the oven rack," she announced.

She wasn't being rational, and he didn't know what he could do for her here. The only thing he could think of was to take her to the nearest emergency room, a good twenty-minute drive from Apple Grove.

"It can wait. I'm taking you to County General."

"Scott, I'm only a little skinned up. I used to get worse scrapes than this falling off my bike. Just let my head clear."

"You always were a lousy bike rider, but you didn't fall on anything as filthy as that cellar floor. You're going to the emergency room."

Her resistance crumpled, a sure sign that she really was hurt. He helped her off the counter and supported her for the walk to his truck.

"I need to wash up. I can't go anywhere like this," she told him.

He laughed softly. This was also the Lori he knew, always wanting to look and be the best she could. Unfortunately, this was one time when they would do things his way. Blood was still soaking one leg of her jeans, and he was sure her injuries were beyond anything he could help with the small first-aid kit in his tool chest.

* * *

The trip seemed longer today, but he made good time. This wasn't his first trip to the emergency room, so Scott knew exactly where to go. Joey had given him a real scare a year or so ago, when he had trouble breathing. It turned out that he had allergies and was particularly sensitive to the budding of trees in the spring. Scott also knew from experience that it could be a long wait before a doctor would see Lori.

She walked stiff legged but unaided to the waiting area, resisting his suggestion that he get a wheelchair.

"I really don't need to be here," she whispered after he signed her in. "I can take care of myself with some soap and water."

"We're here now," he said.

He was no stranger to cuts and bruises, and her one knee looked bad, still oozing blood.

She pretended to read a magazine, but he noticed that she didn't turn the page. He sat silently beside her for what seemed like ages; then he started pacing restlessly in the confines of the waiting area.

"Scott, why don't you go back to work? I'll find a way to get home."

"And wait until your aunt gets through teaching? You don't want to do that."

"Maybe a taxi."

"Have you ever seen a cab in Apple Grove?"

"There must be one somewhere in the county."

"You could order a limo from Des Moines."

He hadn't meant to be sarcastic, but it had slipped out. Lori was smart, the sharpest girl he'd ever had as a friend, but sometimes she got bogged down in wishful thinking—like her crusade to convert him when they were in high school.

He checked with the woman on duty at the reception desk, but she wasn't sure when Lori would be seen.

"What did she say?" Lori asked.

He slumped down beside her and shrugged his shoulders. He could ill afford to miss a whole day of work. The committee was eager to see progress at the café, but he pressured himself even more than they did. No work, no pay, and there were always bills due. He had to write a check for day care by Friday, or look for someone else to take care of Joey. Hopefully, he'd get paid for building the wheelchair ramp by then, or the two of them would be eating boxed macaroni and cheese for a week.

"Your turn is next, but they're still working on someone who had a heart attack."

"That's what emergency rooms are for. I feel foolish sitting here with skinned knees."

He didn't have an answer. At least she still had insurance from her last job, although she said that she was worried because it would expire soon. He knew what it was like to raise a child with only minimum coverage for serious emergencies.

At last a gray-haired nurse in bright purple scrubs pushed a wheelchair over to Lori.

"I don't need that," Lori protested.

"Indulge me," the woman said with a smile. "It's how I get my exercise."

Lori limped to the wheelchair, probably a little surprised at how stiff her knees had gotten while she sat waiting.

"You coming?" the nurse asked him.

"No," Lori said emphatically.

There were three curtained cubicles, and the nurse wheeled Lori to the third one in the row, then helped her onto an examining table.

"Looks like you've been roller-skating," the nurse said lightheartedly.

"No, nothing fun like that. A step collapsed, and I landed on the cellar floor. I really didn't think it was serious enough to come here, but my friend insisted."

"You have a good friend. Do you mind it I cut off the legs of your jeans?" the nurse asked.

"No, I don't see any way of salvaging them."

The cold steel of the scissors on her thighs made Lori shiver, and it hurt a lot when the nurse carefully peeled away the bloody material stuck to the wounds.

Lori gritted her teeth and prayed for the strength not to act like a baby as the nurse professionally cleaned both her knees and palms. The doctor, a young, bearded man with a pleasantly soothing voice, came in and approved of the treatment so far.

"I didn't want to come here," Lori repeated for his benefit, feeling self-conscious about all the attention she was getting.

"Good thing you did," he said. "When did you last have a tetanus shot?"

"Maybe when I was a kid. I'm not sure."

"Better have one now," the doctor advised.

Cold fingers of dread distracted her from the pain in her hands and knees. She hated shots, loathed them.

"Is it really necessary?"

"That would be a yes." The doctor seemed to be enjoying himself. Maybe it was a relief for him to work on something that wasn't life threatening.

She thought of a sharp needle sinking into her soft flesh. She dreaded it the way some people feared snakebites. It was illogical, but maybe all phobias were. Should she ask for a tranquilizer first? Or just refuse? After all, they wouldn't tie her to the table and force her to get a shot.

Dear Lord, if this is what I need, please give me the strength to accept it with dignity and thankfulness, she prayed to herself.

She was making a big deal of a very small thing. Little babies and toddlers got shots with less fuss than she felt like creating.

The doctor left, but the nurse went about some preparations behind Lori's back. Lori cringed when she saw what was in the nurse's hand. That needle was meant for her.

How long could it take to patch up a few scrapes? Scott left the waiting area and found a vending machine that sold cups of a black substance that could just barely pass as coffee. He drank it while standing in the corridor, then hurried back, hoping Lori would be ready to go.

He was a little surprised to realize that he was worried about her, not about getting back to work. In fact, she was on his mind a lot lately, and that couldn't be good. He could easily fall for her again, but they didn't have any more of a future now than they'd had years ago, especially since she was definitely leaving in a few months.

At long last she did return, still in the wheelchair. She looked pale and shaken, her eyes shadowed and her lips clenched. For one horrible moment, he thought there must be something drastically wrong with her.

"Are you okay?" he asked, taking control of the wheelchair and pushing her toward the exit.

"I didn't bargain on a tetanus shot."

"Good thing you had one. That floor was filthy."

"Easy for you to say! I hate shots!"

He laughed, probably the wrong thing to do.

"I've always hated needles. I can't even stand to sew up a turkey."

"I guess a lot of people feel that way," he said sympathetically. "Do you want a soda or something before we start back?"

"No, thank you. I just want to go home."

He badly wanted to do something to soothe her, make her feel better, but he felt helpless.

He settled her into the truck, but before he could return the wheelchair, his cell phone rang. He always answered it with trepidation, worried that it could be about Joey. This time he was right.

He listened, frowning. Could the day get any worse?

Before he started the truck to leave, he told Lori the bad news.

"Joey threw up at day care."

Chapter Seven

Scott took a shortcut back to town, driving the truck as fast as the gravel road would allow.

"Do you think Joey has stomach flu?" she asked, with concern.

"Unlikely," he said wearily. "Sometimes he gets a little nauseous from his allergies. I'm afraid I'll have to pick him up before I take you home."

"No problem, Scott," she assured him.

Lori looked out the window, finding the landscape calming. Growing up in Iowa, she'd never fully appreciated the rich dark earth or the bountiful corn and soybean crops that sprang up every year. Now she could see God's hand all around her, and she wondered what His purpose was in bringing her back here for the summer.

Now that her decision was made, she was having second thoughts. She had lots of friends in Chicago, but most lived miles away from her new job, city miles with a sea of cars, making it very time consuming to visit back and forth. Taking the job pretty much meant starting over from scratch.

She'd been homesick when she'd first left Apple Grove and again when her job frustrations had grown unbearable. Would she experience the same longing for familiar faces and places when she got back to the Chicago area?

Would it be as hard to get over Scott now as it had been the first time she'd left? She stole a brief glance in his direction and felt her heart constrict. She'd resisted caring too much for him when she'd thought he was still with his wife. Now all her defenses had crumbled. His strength made her wish for someone to lean on. His kindness made her yearn to overlook their differences.

She shook her head to chase away her errant thoughts. It gave her a peace of sorts to know her decision had been made. She was getting what she'd always wanted, a chance to work her way up to the position of head chef in a gourmet restaurant. It was her reason for defying her parents and going to cooking school, instead of getting a college degree to teach. If she stayed in Apple Grove, there was no guarantee that she and Scott wouldn't drift apart. They had little in common. Without the café renovations, no doubt they wouldn't have spent any time together.

"How're you doing?" Scott asked, breaking into her thoughts.

"Oh, I'll be fine. I'm just embarrassed for being so silly about the shot."

This wasn't entirely true. Her knees and palms throbbed with pain. She was hard put to decide where it hurt the most, but it was her decision to leave Apple

Grove that disturbed her the most. What if she was making a big mistake?

"I imagine doctors see that a lot," he said. "Don't let it bother you."

They lapsed into a companionable silence, and she was glad he'd shown so much concern for her injuries.

"Wait here. I'll just be a minute," he said, stopping the truck in front of a neat brick house with a high board fence around the backyard.

Betty Drummond had run the town's only licensed day care for a dozen or more years, and Lori knew her casually from church. She'd never struck Lori as a very warm or outgoing person, but the working parents in town appreciated having a safe, orderly place to leave their children.

She watched Scott hurry to the side entrance and wait for someone to come to the door. He didn't need to go in. Joey was ushered out immediately, with his little backpack. He was talking earnestly to his father, looking more agitated than sick, as they walked to the truck.

"Lori had a bad morning, too," Scott explained to his son as he boosted him into his car seat. "She fell down the steps and had to go to the emergency room."

"And I had to have a shot," she added.

"Do I have to go to the 'mergency room and have a shot?" Joey asked, with alarm. "I hate shots."

"No, of course not," Scott reassured him. "You and I know that your allergies make your tummy upset sometimes."

"Mrs. Drummond said I have to go home when I throw up," Joey added.

"Well, that's where you're going as soon as I drop Lori off," said Scott.

"I have an idea," Lori said slowly. "I won't get any more work done today, but I surely can sit. If you'll rinse that last oven rack with vinegar—there's plenty in the café kitchen—I'd be happy to stay with Joey so you can go back to work."

Joey squealed with pleasure and began babbling about the games he wanted to play with Lori.

Scott didn't say anything.

Lori looked over at him. "If you don't think it's a good idea…"

"No, it's fine. It just seems like a lot to ask of you after your fall."

"We both want the same thing—to get the café up and running as soon as possible," she said.

"Thank you for offering," Scott said. "I appreciate it."

It was only a short drive to the trailer park. It had been on the north side of Apple Grove for as long as Lori could remember, and one of her cheerleading friends had lived there with her single mom. The place had a settled look, unlike the campground atmosphere of earlier years. Some of the trailers had colorful canopies and outdoor furniture, while others had small garden areas or pots for flowers.

Scott stopped the truck in front of a weathered green-and-white trailer with none of the amenities of the others.

"Stay there. I'll help you down," he said. "Just let me get Joey out first."

Lori nodded. "Here's the key," he said, handing a key ring to his son as soon as he was on the ground. "Show Lori how you can unlock the door all by yourself."

Joey ran up to the door, and Scott came around to the passenger side of the truck.

"Your offer was well-meant," he said in a somber

voice, "but I'd rather you run ideas past me before letting Joey hear."

"If you don't want me to…"

"That's not what I'm saying. I just like to make decisions about Joey before he gets excited about them."

"I understand," she said, surprised at how much his words hurt. She'd only wanted to be helpful.

She waved aside his hand when he tried to help her down and limped up to the open door where Joey was happily waving the key.

"If Joey is hungry later, he can have a peanut butter sandwich. Afraid there's not much in the house, but help yourself to whatever you can find. I should be able to finish pulling down the walls before six. I'll call if I'm going to be later."

"I'm not in a hurry," she said.

"You'd better give me your cell number. I'll write mine down for you. Call me if Joey is sick again, but usually he feels better after throwing up once. There are some emergency numbers stuck on the fridge."

"Don't worry, Scott. I used to babysit a lot."

"I'm not a baby," Joey emphatically reminded her.

Scott found a pad in a kitchen drawer, wrote his cell number quickly and passed a sheet to her. Once they'd exchanged numbers, he tousled Joey's fine blond hair and left without saying anything else to her.

Scott left the trailer, satisfied that Joey would be all right but not sure he would be. How had this happened? From the first moment he'd seen Lori again, he'd resolved not to get too close. He didn't need or want to start anything with her, not even a friendship. He'd suffered enough in high school, wanting to get close to her but rebuffed because he wasn't religious enough. Maybe if he hadn't been so down when she'd left town for good, he might not have gotten together with Mandy....

He shouldn't and couldn't blame Lori for his loveless marriage. Mandy had been pretty and lots of fun in the beginning, but neither of them had been ready for the reality of married life, Mandy even less so than him. It was painful to remember how unhappy she'd been after she'd quit her job to have Joey. She'd felt like a prisoner when she was in the trailer all day with the baby, and she'd tried to make herself happy by going out with friends whenever she had a chance. Their marriage had ended months before the car accident.

He didn't want Joey to be hurt when Lori left town, which was her goal. The more time she spent with him, the more his son was likely to miss her.

He went back to the café, too agitated to worry about lunch. The sooner he ripped out the old walls, the quicker he could get Lori out of his and his son's life.

The only word for Scott's trailer was spartan. It was scrupulously clean, not what she might expect from a bachelor household, but only the bare necessities took up space in the rather cramped interior. The only cheer came from Joey's bright bedspread with dancing dinosaurs and his well-stocked toy box.

"Well, what would you like to do?" she asked the little boy as soon as his father drove away.

"Play games!" he was quick to answer, throwing open a cupboard and rummaging through a pile of board games. "I like this one best."

He carried it to the kitchen counter and climbed up on a stool. Lori sat opposite and resigned herself to moving plastic pieces around a board with brightly colored squares for the next hour. Joey had an amazing attention span, or so it seemed to her. At least he hadn't asked her to play anything that involved sitting on the floor. Her knees hurt so much that she doubted whether she could get up again, and she'd completely forgotten about the prescription she had to fill at the pharmacy.

When Joey won his third game in a row, she realized that it was past lunchtime.

"Did you have lunch at day care?" she asked.

"No, Mrs. D. didn't want me to throw up again."

"Would you like something now?"

He nodded his head, apparently willing but not particularly eager.

Lori hobbled over to the small refrigerator and found little of interest. There was a half-eaten loaf of bread and a carton of eggs. Fortunately, there was also a stick of margarine. She was inspired.

"Have you ever had eggs in a basket?" she asked, finally piquing Joey's interest in food.

Together they cut circles out of two bread slices with the edge of a juice glass, put both slices in heated margarine in a skillet and cracked an egg into the hole in each slice. She served the dish with the cutout bread circle on top of the egg as a cover, and Joey was so enchanted that he insisted on making a second one for himself.

"My daddy doesn't make these," he said, wiping egg yolk from his mouth.

"Now you can teach him how," Lori said, glad that her babysitting venture wasn't a failure.

Scott called around four to see if everything was okay. It was, and he promised to be home by six. Lori called her aunt and explained the situation, asking if she would mind picking her up. She didn't want to be obliged to Scott for a ride home.

It was a long day that ended with Joey cuddled beside her on the couch while she read some of his favorite books aloud.

Scott was bone weary by the time he'd stripped the walls down to the studs and hauled the debris to the dump, exhausted, filthy and hungry. He'd been so eager to get back to work that he'd skipped lunch. Too bad there wasn't a functioning restaurant in town. He'd give a day's pay for one of Amos Conklin's famous chicken dinners with all the fixings, but it would be a while before the Highway Café was back in business.

Remembering his empty cupboards and fridge, he stopped at the grocery store for TV dinners, milk and a box of cereal.

He'd have to take Lori home and have a shower before he could even think of eating. Hopefully, Joey wasn't as hungry as he was.

When he pulled up to his trailer, there was an unfamiliar car parked in his usual place. It didn't take him long to figure out that Lori had called her aunt to take her home. No wonder, after he'd chastised her earlier. She had only been trying to do him a favor and hadn't deserved to be put down. The thought that he'd been mean to Lori made him miserable.

At least she hadn't tried to give him any child-rearing advice. He got plenty from Mrs. Drummond at the day care and his sister, Doreen, not to mention every other female who got close enough to bend his ear.

When he stepped into the trailer, the sound of happy chatter died away. Joey was sitting at the counter, with a bowl of macaroni and cheese, enjoying the attention of both Lori and her aunt.

"Sorry I'm late," he said. "Had to stop at the store."

He plunked his two bags of groceries down on the counter beside the stove.

"We've been having a fine time," Bess said. "Joey counted a hundred and two macaroni noodles before we put them in boiling water. I was impressed."

"Lori made me eggs in a basket, Daddy. They were really good," Joey reported. "Can you make them for breakfast tomorrow?"

"You'll have to show me how." Scott avoided looking at Lori but felt he had to say something to her. "Thanks a lot for watching Joey. I got a lot done this afternoon."

"The committee is meeting Wednesday evening. Is there anything I should tell them?" Bess asked.

"Only that I've torn out the old wallboard," Scott told her. "I'm going to fix the cellar steps next. I don't want anyone else falling."

"Good idea," the older woman said.

Lori hadn't said a word since he walked in. Instead, she gave Joey a little hug and limped over to the door, ready to leave.

Scott was about to ask her how she felt, but she didn't give him a chance. She was out the door while Bess was still talking about the committee's hope to get the renovations done quickly.

By the time Scott cleaned up, ate and got Joey settled

for the night, he got his second wind. He wiped off the kitchen counters, mopped the kitchen area and cleaned the bathroom but still felt too restless to watch TV or go to bed. This was the hardest time of day, when Joey was sleeping and he had quiet time to think. Tonight he was plagued by thoughts of what he could have done differently in his life. Lori kept popping into his thoughts against his will.

He picked up his phone and dialed the number she'd given him in case he'd needed to reach her that day.

"Hello?" Her voice sounded sweet and drowsy, and he worried that she'd been sleeping.

"Lori, it's Scott. I hope I didn't wake you."

"Actually, you did. I dozed off while reading a book in the living room, so you've done me a favor. I'd get a stiff neck if I slept in a chair all night."

"I just wondered how you're feeling."

"Stiff, sore and dumb. I never should've gone down those steps. I knew they were old and creaky."

"There was no reason to think one would collapse. I'm going to fix them first thing tomorrow."

"Good, but it will be a long time before I go down in that cellar again."

She laughed lightly, and he remembered that she had the nicest laugh of anyone he'd ever met. That didn't make it any easier to say what he had to say.

"The reason I called," he said, determined to get it over with, "is that I was way out of line, criticizing you for offering to babysit in front of Joey. I hope you'll accept my apology."

"You don't need to apologize, Scott. I can't even imagine how hard it must be raising Joey on your own."

"It's not that hard. I love him a lot. He makes everything I do worthwhile."

He'd said his piece, but somehow it didn't seem like enough. For once he let an impulse take over.

"You helped me a lot, watching Joey so I could get more work done. I wonder if you'd let me thank you by taking you out for dinner Friday. I'm pretty sure I can get a girl who lives near us to babysit. She's only thirteen, but she and Joey have fun together."

"A date?" She sounded puzzled.

"No, just two old friends having dinner to celebrate your new job. It's the least I can do to repay you."

"You took me to the emergency room. Certainly that makes us even."

"If you don't want to go—"

"I didn't say that!"

"Then we have a…" He nearly said "date."

"I think it would be nice if we had dinner. Thanks for asking."

"Okay if I pick you up at seven?"

"Fine. Friday at seven."

He held the phone in his hand for a long time after breaking the connection.

What had he done? And why?

Chapter Eight

With her major career decision made and with time on her hands until the café could open, Lori was excited to start her freelance job testing recipes for a kid-friendly cookbook. Maggie, the author, was a friend from the cooking school they'd both attended in Chicago, and she already had a publisher interested in the cookbook.

Tomorrow Lori was going to dinner with Scott, so tonight was a good time to serve her aunt one of the entrées she needed to test. She scanned the recipes she'd just received in her e-mail and settled on number four. None of the dishes had been named yet as far as she knew, but this chicken recipe suggested a number of snappy names, like Corny Chicken or Sticky Chicken Fillets.

After a trip to the store, she assembled her ingredients: thin strips of skinless, boneless chicken breast, honey, orange juice, cornflakes and seasonings. She rinsed the chicken, then combined her wet and dry ingredients in separate bowls. She wasn't sure about including the amount of pepper called for in the recipe, but Maggie had two young children. No doubt her friend knew more about young children's tolerance for zesty flavors than she did. Lori's job was to critique the recipes as they were, without any alterations.

Maggie was spot-on in estimating that the preparation time was only twelve minutes. Lori actually shaved off a couple of minutes, but then, she was used to working fast in busy kitchens. She brushed the honey–orange juice mixture over the chicken strips, sprinkled on the seasoned cornflakes and popped them into a preheated oven. Baking time was only twenty minutes, just enough for Lori to fix a salad to go with the chicken.

Bess raved about the crunchy chicken when they shared the results of Lori's first recipe test.

"This is good enough to serve in the café," she said, her pet project never far from her mind.

"You and I think it's good," Lori said thoughtfully, "but the whole idea of the cookbook is to fix things young children will like."

"Well, next time you test a recipe, feed it to some children."

"That's a really good idea."

"Joey seemed like a good eater," Bess suggested, slipping into matchmaker mode.

"I was thinking of Sara's daughter, Sunny."

"Use both of them, if their parents agree. After all, two opinions are twice as good as one."

"We'll see," Lori said, still mulling over better ways to test the appeal of the recipes.

After dinner, Bess volunteered to clean up, and Lori went to her room. Staring into the closet, she realized how inadequate her wardrobe was when it came to nice clothes. She'd had her share of dates in Chicago, but she and her roommate had traded back and forth since neither could afford many party clothes.

She'd thought of little else but Scott all week. When she went back to Chicago, she might not see him again for ages, if ever. Of course, she would come back to visit her aunt from time to time, but Scott would go on with his life. He might remarry or even move away if a good opportunity presented itself. This dinner with Scott was more than a celebration of her new job. It was a way of saying goodbye to their shared past, a way for old friends to find closure before the rush of opening the café and packing up to move again.

Her excitement about the evening was tinged with sadness. She was torn between wanting to get on with her life and not wanting to say goodbye to Scott forever.

Well, fortunately, they still had the whole summer. It was only in her imagination that she saw this evening as some kind of farewell party.

Then it struck her. Scott had gone on with his life after she'd left town. He'd married, had a child and settled into a business of his own. She was the one who was stuck in the past, still thinking of him as the high school boy she'd loved.

On Friday, with less than half an hour before he was due, Lori turned her attention to her still-damp hair. It had been unmanageable after she shampooed, so she'd piled it on top of her head and secured it with a set of mock tortoiseshell combs. Then she went back to the closet, still undecided about what to wear. Her black dress was much too formal, and her tweed business suit seemed too prim and proper, not to mention too wintry.

She had no idea where they were going, but it was spring. The day had been unseasonably warm and humid, although that didn't mean much in Iowa. It could be balmy one day and blustery the next.

The longer she dithered over what to wear, the more important the date with Scott seemed. She took one more quick look at the contents of the closet, then grabbed a summer cotton, a pink print with nosegays of flowers in the pattern. She had bought it to go to a friend's wedding and hadn't worn it since because it didn't fit her lifestyle. It still didn't, but this evening was probably a once-in-a-lifetime event. There was no reason to believe that he'd seek out her company again, and she sympathized with his concern about Joey. He couldn't allow his son to get too attached to her, not when she clearly was leaving.

Joey had dozens of questions about where his dad was going and why he couldn't go, too. Scott fielded them as best he could, but the truth was that he didn't have all the answers himself. The more he thought about it, the more he questioned his reason for asking Lori to dinner.

"You like Amy," he reminded his son. "She's a good sitter. She'll read stories to you."

"Can I stay up until you get home?"

"Okay, but I want you in your pajamas, with your teeth brushed, when I get back. Deal?"

"Deal." Joey gave him a high five, then settled down to watch as Scott tied his tie in the bathroom mirror.

He hardly recognized himself in his summer-weight

tan sports jacket and dress slacks, not to mention a white shirt and brown-and-tan striped tie. In fact, he couldn't remember when he'd last dressed up—maybe when he'd applied for a loan at the bank to buy his second-hand truck.

His slacks felt a little loose around the waist, so he tightened the belt a notch. He must have lost weight, not surprising since most of his meals were geared to Joey's taste.

What did he expect to come of asking Lori out? He'd asked himself that question a hundred times, and the answer was always the same: nothing. If they couldn't connect in high school, they certainly couldn't have any kind of a relationship now that she'd decided to leave again. They were farther apart than the north and south poles. If it weren't for the work he was doing at the café, they probably wouldn't have spoken more than three words to each other the whole time she'd been in town.

Opening the door to watch for the sitter, he saw her hurry past the three trailers that separated her home from his. Amy was a few minutes early, but he was grateful. The sooner he picked up Lori, the more relaxed he would feel. He felt like a kid on his first date, which was ridiculous.

He worried what they would talk about. Once, they'd been able to spend hours talking about their lives and what they hoped to make of them. He had no idea what they'd talk about now.

He was out in his truck, ready to leave, when he admitted to himself that he was more than a little nervous. He was way out of practice when it came to the dating scene, and never in his wildest imagination would he have dreamed he'd be picking up Lori for an evening out.

Of course, it wasn't really a date, but just two old friends having dinner.

He pulled up in front of Bess's house, and Lori stepped out onto the porch before he could get out of the truck.

"Hi," he said, hurrying to open the passenger door for her.

"Hi."

He helped her up, trying to think of something clever—or even halfway interesting—to say. He drew a blank, then remembered her accident.

"How are your knees?"

"Coming along fine."

"Your hands?"

"Healing nicely. And I didn't have a bad reaction from the shot, silly as I was about getting one."

"I wasn't going to mention it." He smiled, then started the truck and kept his eyes glued to the street ahead.

He turned around in a neighbor's driveway, gunning the truck more than necessary when he backed out.

"It was nice of you to ask me to dinner. Aunt Bess has been promising—make that threatening—to make her infamous tuna casserole. It beats me where she got the idea of crumbling vanilla wafers on top."

They both laughed, and it felt amazingly good.

"I'd take you to the best restaurant in town, but the soda fountain in the drugstore closes at six," he teased.

"That will change when the café is up and running."

"Are you going to serve good old-fashioned meals that stick to the ribs?"

"You'll have to wait and see," she said, grinning at him.

"Fair enough. Gives me more incentive to get the work done as fast as I can."

"Where are we going, if you don't mind my asking?"

"Benedict."

"Benedict? That has to be the smallest town in Iowa. Do they have a restaurant?"

"Hope so. Otherwise, we have a reservation for dinner nowhere."

"A reservation? That sounds impressive. I don't remember much being there except a grain elevator and a roller-skating rink."

"I helped renovate an old house for the restaurant owners. They live upstairs. It's a retirement business for them, but they're getting a good reputation."

Glancing sideways at her, he admired the way her hair was piled high on her head. One strand had escaped, and his fingers itched to touch it. He'd always thought she had the prettiest hair he'd ever seen. He was glad she hadn't dyed it blond or chopped it short.

They talked about Joey and the café and Bess, and the drive to Benedict didn't seem that long at all. He was relieved that she didn't ask anything about his wife, but the Lori he knew was always tactful and considerate. Maybe someday…

It didn't seem real, sitting beside Lori in the confines of the cab, talking as though they hadn't been separated for years. It felt right, and that scared him. There was no place he'd rather be, and no one he'd rather have beside him, but it could lead only to a world of hurt when she finally left at the end of the summer.

He clenched the wheel so hard, his fingers hurt, and he tried to engage in lighthearted chatter. He was way out of practice. By the time they reached the restaurant, they'd both fallen silent.

Hopefully, the place would be busy and noisy, too noisy for any conversation that would let her know how much he didn't want her to leave Apple Grove. He could point out the renovations he'd done there and focus on what had to be done at the café. The evening would go too quickly, and he suspected he would want it to go on and on. This might be the only chance he'd have to be alone with Lori, and he wanted it to be a good memory. He had more than enough bad ones.

Lori clenched her jaw to keep her teeth from chattering, a nervous tic that betrayed her excitement at being with Scott. It had nothing to do with the cool evening breeze coming in through the truck window. In fact, she had brought her white sweater but felt no need to slip into it.

The parking area beside the restaurant was still well lit by the setting sun, and she noticed how nicely Scott had dressed when he walked around the front of the truck to open the door for her. She couldn't remember when, if ever, she'd seen him in a jacket and tie. It made her wish she'd gone with the black dress. She was pretty sure this would be a one-time opportunity to be out with him, and that made her sadder than she would have dreamed possible.

"If you think the café is a mess, you should have seen this place before it was renovated," he said, offering his hand so she could slip down.

"Did you do the whole job?"

She looked at the large wood-frame house, which was typical of many Iowa homes built in the early nineteen hundreds. The narrow wooden siding was smooth and freshly painted a cheerful yellow, and lace curtains softened the severe lines of the windows. The only sign that it was a restaurant was a small bronze plaque by the front door.

"No, it took a whole crew. I don't have the time or patience to do jobs like sanding and painting the siding. I was the general contractor, but I called on an electrician, some plumbers and a couple of carpenters to help."

"Are you going to get other workmen to help with the café?"

"I have someone lined up to do the rewiring, but everyone is busy now that spring is here. Here we did most of the interior in the winter, when construction work is harder to come by."

When they walked inside, the first word that came to Lori's mind was *cozy*. Instead of one large dining area, the owners had used the original layout for a series of small, semiprivate serving rooms. There was a comfortable buzz of conversation in the front room, where linen-covered tables were lit by candles in glass lanterns. All the tables were occupied, certainly a good sign in a new restaurant.

"Scott, it's good to see you." A slender woman with coal-black hair pulled into a bun came up to greet them.

"Doris, the place looks great," Scott said.

"And thanks to you, we were up and running for Easter and Mother's Day," Doris said.

"Doris, this is an old friend of mine, Lori Raymond. She's a professional chef."

"How wonderful. Barney will love showing off for someone who can really appreciate his cooking," Doris said.

"Her husband is the chef here," Scott explained.

"I reserved a nice table for you in the little room," Doris said.

"Little room?" Lori asked in a soft voice as they followed her.

"No one could figure out what the room was originally used for, so we started calling it the little room. I guess the name stuck," Scott said.

The room was indeed small. There was room for only one table for two, and Lori was struck by how romantic it was. There were valentine-red brocade wall coverings above the dark wainscoting and several prints of dreamy looking couples from the early twentieth century.

"Karen will be your server," Doris said as she handed them one-page menus. "We're pretty busy tonight, but she'll be here in a few minutes."

"We're not in any hurry," Scott said, giving Lori a warm smile.

"This is really lovely," Lori said once Doris had left them.

"Nice, isn't it? I've been wanting to see how they're doing, but it's not a place to take Joey."

"You've never eaten here?"

"Nope."

The room seemed like an enchanted bower. She loved this feeling of intimacy, of having the other diners present only as a distant hum.

"It has a special ambiance, something out of the ordinary. A lot of restaurants try for it, but not many achieve it," she said.

"Is that your professional opinion?" he asked, grinning broadly to show that he was teasing.

"No, that's your date's opinion."

She felt a warm glow that had nothing to do with their surroundings.

Soft music was piped into the room, dreamy dance tunes that she didn't recognize but that seemed exactly right for her mood.

"Shall we?" he asked as though reading her mind.

"Dance?" She looked around the small room, which was not filled with tables and chairs, and nodded her assent.

"We did miss the prom," he said softly, rising to pull back her chair.

The space was so limited that every step brought them close to banging into a chair or the wall. But Scott held her close, and they danced without collisions. Lori caught a glimpse of a face in the doorway, a waitress, who quickly disappeared instead of coming into the room.

Gradually, the room and the world seemed to dissolve, until they were alone together, moving slowly and totally focused on each other. It was a moment she'd dreamed of years ago, and it felt more wonderful than she could have imagined.

Time was suspended; then reality intruded when Scott backed into a chair and knocked it to the floor. They both dissolved into laughter.

He picked it up, and the mood was broken. Still, Lori felt as though they'd shared a moment of wonder and delight. They sat down across from each other, their eyes locked, almost forgetting that they'd come for a meal.

"Are you folks ready to order?" A stocky young waitress bustled into the room, with water glasses on a tray. What she lacked in poise, she more than made up for in her bright smile and friendly tone.

"I think we need a little more time," Scott said.

There were only six entrées, a wise menu for a small family-run restaurant, but they impressed Lori. They had a choice of stuffed pork chops, an Iowa favorite, beef Stroganoff and filet mignon. The fish dish was rainbow trout, and the special of the day was shepherd's pie.

"Reminds me of how tired I am of my own cooking," Scott said, with a sheepish grin.

"What does Joey like to eat?" she asked him.

"Peanut butter, macaroni and cheese, stuff like that. Why do you ask?"

"I'm testing some recipes geared to children's tastes. A friend is writing a cookbook. I made a chicken recipe for Aunt Bess and me, but we're really not qualified to say whether kids would like it. I wondered if I could use Joey as my test subject sometime. I'll probably ask Sara if her little girl can participate, too."

"Sounds fine with me," he said. "It won't hurt your feelings if he hates everything you make, will it?"

"No," she said, laughing. "That's the whole object of the book, making things even picky eaters will enjoy."

She looked into his eyes; the deep blue depths concealed more than they gave away.

"I'm staring. Sorry," he said.

"I guess it's hard not to when we're sitting across from each other," she said, afraid he was being polite because she was the one who'd been staring.

The young waitress came back, her face pink from exertion and her blond ponytail bobbing, and took out her order pad.

"Let's start with an appetizer plate, crab puffs, cheese straws and deep fried-zucchini," Scott said, looking at Lori for approval. "What would you like for an entrée?"

"Oh!" She'd been so distracted by Scott that she hadn't given it any thought.

"You can fill our appetizer order and come back," Scott told their waitress.

"No, we can order now," Lori quickly said. "I'll have the trout, baby green beans and wild rice."

Scott ordered the stuffed pork chop, cottage-fried potatoes and a salad with house dressing.

In spite of Lori's earlier belief that this was just a casual dinner with an old friend, the evening was taking on a whole new dimension. She looked across at Scott and felt something new and totally different than anything else in her experience. He was a beautiful man, the faint lines by his eyes adding maturity without distracting from the impact he was making on her heart. She'd always loved his high cheekbones and strong chin, and she gave herself a moment to enjoy his faint grin, which made her feel all shivery again.

"How is Joey doing in day care?" she asked after searching her mind for something to say that wouldn't reveal her inner turbulence.

It was the right thing to bring up. Scott became animated, telling her about his young son and all the cute things he did.

She took a deep breath, surrendering to the sheer pleasure of being with him.

When the platter of appetizers came, he seemed to enjoy watching her nibble on the food more than he did eating it himself. They couldn't talk with mouths full of crab puff, but their eyes were communicating in a way that went beyond any conversation they'd had.

Scott was neither surprised nor displeased when Lori bowed her head to say grace before beginning to eat. He admired her faith and the open display of it as she prayed silently for several moments. He wished she felt comfortable enough with him to pray aloud.

Her faith was an integral part of who she was. He'd never wanted to dissuade her in any way, not even when they were young. Back then, he'd wished—he'd even prayed, though he'd never told her—that he could feel some of the fervor she felt for the Lord. If faith was a gift, it was one he'd never been given.

Even as a kid, he'd decided not to fake it. He wouldn't go to church and be a hypocrite, pretending to believe to win her approval. No matter how sweet it would have been to hold her in his arms, he couldn't be something he wasn't. Nor would he ever want her to change because of him.

She was even more beautiful on the inside than the outside. She'd grown from a pretty girl to a beautiful woman without losing herself in the process. She was kind, generous, understanding, considerate—all the things Mandy hadn't understood and had never been.

What a mess he'd made of his life. He was a single dad with no social life. He'd made a bad mistake in marrying Mandy, realizing too late that what they shared wasn't a love that was destined to last. But he did have his son. Joey made up for a lot, but being with Lori made him realize that there was still an empty spot in his heart, a yearning that seemed as hopeless as it was intense.

Their entrées came, and he could see how impressed

Lori was by the quality. She praised the chef and the freshness of the ingredients. He agreed, but it was her enthusiasm and her very presence that made the meal so special.

Lori gave the owners high marks for both the service and the food. Their waitress timed her trips to their table beautifully, and when she brought their entrées, she skillfully removed the head of the trout at Lori's request.

"I'm not picky as a rule, but I prefer not to have my dinner looking at me," Lori said with a girlish giggle that reminded him of the times they'd sat talking on her aunt's porch.

When he thought back to his high school days, his clearest memories always seemed to involve her. He remembered searching the stands when he played football, hoping for a glimpse of her. He'd tried to time his arrival at school in the morning so he could talk to her for a few minutes before class. He'd asked her out a few times without success, becoming the object of his friends' jokes, since he could have dated any other girl in the school if he'd wanted to. They took to calling her St. Lori behind her back, and he'd got in more than one fight when he objected.

"Is something wrong?" she asked.

Yes, you're leaving me again, he wanted to say.

He realized that he had cut into his chop and was holding a bite on his fork, forgetting to carry it to his mouth.

"No, it's great." He hurriedly bit into the morsel. "Lots of sage. Delicious. Here. Try a bite. Give me your professional opinion."

"All right."

She opened her mouth, and he carefully fed her a bit of pork and stuffing. It'd been a few years since he'd had to feed Joey, and this was nothing like that.

"That is wonderful!" she exclaimed. "Here. Try my trout."

She pushed her plate toward him, and he was sorry she didn't reciprocate by feeding him. He took a small bite of the trout and nodded his approval, even though fish wasn't one of his favorite foods.

She talked about living in Chicago and made him laugh when she described the pretentious head chef who'd been her boss. She made him sound so overbearing and unfair that Scott had to admire her for sticking it out as long as she had. He couldn't imagine anyone not appreciating her, but he was content to listen without comment.

They lingered over dessert, homemade blueberry pie for him and pineapple sherbet for her. A born hostess, Doris came by to make sure they'd enjoyed the meal. She had that twinkle in her eye that Scott had come to recognize as the matchmaker's hallmark, which was confirmed when she urged them both to come back soon. He wanted that to happen far more than Doris could guess, but then a black moment crept over him. This was a goodbye dinner as much as a celebration. Of course, he'd see more of Lori over the course of the summer, but nothing would ever be as good as this evening.

They didn't talk much on the way home, but it was a companionable silence. Being with Lori felt as natural as breathing, and he tried not to regret that nothing could come of it.

When he parked outside her aunt's house, she started to open the truck door herself.

"Wait a second. I'll get it," he told her.

She hadn't mentioned it, but she still walked stiff legged from the fall.

He took her hand to help her down but quickly released it when her feet were on the ground. It felt much too good to have her small, warm fingers engulfed in his, and he had to remind himself once again that she was going to leave.

She thanked him profusely for the lovely dinner. Frankly, he couldn't even remember what he'd eaten.

"I'm glad you enjoyed it. Thank you for coming with me," he said.

They both stood in the dim light of the porch, not saying a word, neither one of them able to move. Scott stepped closer to her, took her hand in his and kissed the back of it. Lori smiled and left her hand in his for several moments.

"Well, good night," she said softly, finally stepping into the house.

He got in his truck, and drove a bit too fast going home, telling himself that Joey was waiting up, and it was past his bedtime. But no matter how hard he tried to focus on his son, he kept replaying the entire evening in his mind.

Chapter Nine

"Can we go see the bunny rabbit, Daddy?"

Joey was dawdling over his cereal, in no hurry to get to day care.

"I kinda think we have to wait for Miss Bess to invite us, sport."

"Well, when is she going to invite us? She said I could come play again."

"You never know what a woman will do."

It was good to remind himself of that, but it was no comfort to his son.

"But she said!" Joey said emphatically.

Scott sighed and gave the answer that no kid ever bought. "We'll see."

He'd thought of getting a pet for Joey, but his son's allergies always gave him pause. He'd have to go through a whole battery of tests to see what animal, if any, wouldn't trigger a reaction. Then there was the problem of leaving it alone all day. He'd love a dog himself, maybe a beagle or a spaniel, although a nice friendly mutt from the shelter might be a good companion. The trouble with that was an adult dog might come with some bad habits, and a puppy was almost as much work as a baby.

He tabled that thought and urged Joey to finish his breakfast.

"You could call and ask," Joey said. When his son got an idea into his head, he was like a pit bull with a new toy.

"No, now finish your orange juice."

Joey pouted but did as he was told. If Scott were a praying man, he would thank God for blessing him with such a great kid.

Nearly a week had passed since he'd taken Lori out for dinner, and he remembered every minute of it. Especially when he'd kissed her hand. She was constantly on his mind. He'd picked up the phone to call her umpteen times, but for some reason he'd always changed his mind. He wanted to urge her to stay in Apple Grove, but how could he ask her to give up a job that meant a lot to her when there was nothing comparable anywhere near here?

"Daddy, I can't find my Dizzy!"

"We don't have time to look for your dinosaur now. Anyway, Mrs. Drummond doesn't want you to bring toys unless you're willing to share them with the other kids."

"He's mine!"

Obviously, Joey had a lot to learn about sharing, but Scott didn't have time to explain again now. He was taking Joey's hand to lead him to the truck when his cell phone rang.

"Scott, it's Lori."

"Hey! How are you?" He was surprised by the jolt of happiness that coursed through him.

"Fine. Remember when I asked if it would be all right to use Joey as a taste tester for the recipes I'm trying?"

"Sure do."

"Well, I'm going to make some munchies today. I wondered if the two of you could stop by on your way home from day care. I don't think a sample will spoil Joey's dinner, and I'd really appreciate his input."

"Sure. We'd be glad to," he quickly agreed.

"Oh, I have some samples of the building materials that the committee approved, too. I hope you'll like them."

"If you like them, I'm sure I will, too."

"See you later, then. Bye, Scott."

The more Lori thought about it, the more she didn't want to wait until late afternoon to give Scott the samples the committee members had selected. They'd picked warm butternut siding, not real wood but an attractive facsimile, and a linoleum pattern that resembled ceramic tile but was considerably less expensive. At this point, they were all about saving money and getting the job done quickly so the café could open. Many of the backers were retired and were eager to get some return on their investments.

Scott hadn't called her after their wonderful date, a disappointment, but she understood how busy he was with work and Joey. She prayed that someday he would come to know the Lord, for Joey's sake as much as his own, but she was unhappily resigned that she and Scott would go their separate ways.

She should have been excited about the prospect of going back to Chicago, but Scott was constantly on her mind, making her question her decision.

Then there was Joey. He was a miniature version of his father, and she adored him. When she thought of the way he'd cuddled beside her to listen to stories, her heart melted. She prayed for him, too, wondering whether Sunday-school lessons were enough to teach him to love the Lord.

It was a fair day, warm and breezy, with the wind carrying the sweet perfume of flowering bushes. Her knees had healed enough to make walking comfortable, so she started off for the café. Their dinner together had changed things between them, and she was nervous about seeing Scott again. How much would the wonder of that evening carry over into the harsher light of day?

All she really had to do was hand him the samples and tell him the committee's decisions. She could be in and out of there in two minutes, but she tried to think of reasons to stay longer. It was a joy to watch him at work. He used an economy of motion that showed how skilled he was. He always seemed to know exactly what to do.

As she walked to the café, she tried to think of something clever to say when she got there, but it was hopeless. She wanted to tell him how wonderful the evening out had been and how happy it had made her to be with him, but words failed her.

She heard him before she saw him. The café door was open, letting spring air into the dusty interior, and he was working back in the kitchen area. She walked through the space where he'd removed the swinging doors and saw him on his knees in front of the storage shelves. He didn't hear her, and she stood a moment, watching as he worked. Moist tendrils of hair clung to the back of his neck, and she had to resist the urge to touch them.

"Hi, Scott."

He looked up, startled by Lori's sudden appearance. "Hi."

He stood, pleased and surprised to see her. She hadn't been to the café all week, and he'd missed seeing her more than he would have thought possible just a few short weeks ago.

"It's such a nice day for a walk that I decided to bring the samples of the materials the committee members chose."

"Good. I need to order anything that isn't in stock."

He reached for the little samples she was holding out, conscious of how grubby he was. This was turning into a really dirty job, with decades of accumulated dirt and rot to contend with. He'd be glad when all he had to do was put in new materials.

"I think they made good choices, with an emphasis on economy, but these materials are still light and pleasant," she said.

"The café never was a fancy place."

"You really did a great job on the restaurant—where we went the other night."

"Thanks."

"Thank you again for taking me there. It was a lovely evening."

He pulled off his work gloves and took a long swig from the water bottle he'd brought with him. It would take more than a moment's pause to know how to answer her.

"I enjoyed it, too," he said, thinking how beautiful

she'd looked sitting across from him. "Maybe we can go there again before you leave," he added, knowing no good could come of it. The more time he spent with her, the harder it would be to see her go.

"Yes, that would be nice," she replied.

He could hear blood thundering in his ears like an approaching storm. He was dirty, sweaty and dejected, hardly someone who would appeal to a lovely woman like Lori. Would she really like to go on another date, or was she only being polite? This wasn't the time or the place for a serious conversation, and he didn't want to give her a chance to reject him. He wasn't a high school kid anymore who could have his pick of any girl in the school. He couldn't think of one reason why a woman with prospects like Lori's would want to bother with him.

"We'll stay good friends, I hope," he said.

"Yes."

"I guess it's funny how our lives have changed, but some things have stayed the same."

"I should be going," she said. "I know how much you have to do here. You're still going to stop by with Joey, aren't you?"

"Sure. Do I get to be a taste tester, too?"

"I'd love to have your opinion."

"Joey was excited when I told him. He thinks a lot of you. I'm afraid he'll really miss you when you leave."

What he said was true, but it was only a partial truth. He was the one who was most vulnerable. Now that he'd let himself get close to her, it would be like ripping his heart out when she left.

She nodded. "The last thing I want is to cause Joey any pain. If you think it would be better that…"

"We don't see too much of each other," he said before she could finish her sentence.

"That's what I was going to say," she said.

He could hear sadness in her voice and hurried to assure her that both he and Joey wanted to see as much of her as they could. For a moment he was afraid she was going to cry. If she did, he wouldn't be able to stop himself from taking her in his arms.

"I'd better go," she said, backing away from him.

"Thanks for the samples. I'll order the materials we need today."

"Good. I hope to get the café running smoothly before I have to leave."

"It won't be a problem. By the way, I fixed the cellar steps." He was torn between needing her to go quickly and wanting to feast his eyes on her for a few more precious moments.

"Someone from the committee will be coming to clear out the cellar," she said.

"I suppose there must be some salable things down there."

"I guess. It's too creepy for me, though."

"There should be enough storage in the kitchen area when I'm done, so you won't have to go down in the cellar." He wanted to do something to make her smile, but it wasn't as if she'd be working there very long.

"Thanks. I appreciate that." She turned and left with a hasty goodbye.

True to his word, Scott arrived at Bess's house with Joey soon after he picked him up from day care. Lori was ready for them with her newly made snack mix in small bowls on the table, with an extra bag for Joey to take home if he liked it. It was an unusual recipe, using bite-sized pieces of shredded wheat cereal, peanuts, dried fruit and peanut butter, among other ingredients. She wasn't sure about giving peanuts to Joey, but Scott assured her that he could handle them and wasn't allergic.

Scott looked tired, and she was quick to offer him some freshly made coffee.

"How do you like it, Joey?" Lori asked when he'd had a chance to sample the snack.

"It's good," he replied.

She noticed that he was picking out the raisins.

"Are you sure you like it? You don't have to say that you like it just because I made it."

"I don't like these brown things," he said with the refreshing honesty of the very young.

"Would you like it if they weren't in it?" Lori asked.

"Maybe." He nibbled on a bite of shredded wheat, but not very enthusiastically.

"For what it's worth, I think it's great," Scott said, emptying the small bowl she'd set in front of him.

"I guess that makes the score big boys, one, little boys, zero," Lori said.

"Sorry," Scott said, shrugging his shoulders. "I'm afraid Joey's food tastes are pretty limited. Blame his father's lousy cooking."

Lori shook her head. "No, I'm sure other children might feel the same way. My job is to get reactions both positive and negative. Joey, you've been a big help."

When the two of them started to leave, Lori handed the bag of snack mix to Scott. "Maybe you'd like it for your lunch."

"Thanks. It won't go to waste," he promised.

She didn't mind at all that Joey hadn't liked the snack mix. She was only sad to see them go off together, just the two of them, Scott's hand on Joey's shoulder. Even though they had each other, there was a loneliness about them that touched her heart.

The next day Lori desperately needed something to distract her. Just waiting around for the café to be finished would have been hard enough under any circumstances, but if she did nothing but think about Scott, she'd end up in tears.

Instead, she called Sara and suggested they have lunch.

"I have a better idea," Sara said. "I'm home alone—it's my mother-in-law's birthday—but one of us has to be here because an electrician is coming. Come out here, and we can talk until we're hoarse."

"I'd love to."

Half an hour later Lori pulled into the long drive leading to her friend's modern brick home. This wasn't a farm with a sprawl of antiquated outbuildings, but an up-to-date operation with equipment stored in a large utilitarian shed some distance from the house. As far as she could see, newly planted fields of corn were sprouting under a sky that was beginning to darken.

She'd missed the sky when she'd lived in Chicago. Of course, the Windy City had one, but the vistas were never so awe inspiring. From where she was standing, Lori could see the curvature of the earth and the weather front moving in from the west. She felt more a part of God's creation here than anywhere else, and she took a few moments to pray for a tranquil spirit and guidance in her life.

Calmer than when she'd left her aunt's house, Lori walked up to the front door where her friend was waiting to welcome her.

"I am so super happy to have you back," Sara said, hugging her exuberantly. "I wish you weren't planning to leave after Labor Day, but, of course, you have too much talent for Apple Grove."

"I don't know about that, but there are more opportunities in a big city."

"I always thought I'd be the one to leave here," Sara said.

"I never saw you as a farmer's wife." Lori followed her friend to a modern kitchen with stainless-steel appliances and granite counters.

"Me either, but what's a girl to do? You marry a lifestyle along with a man, and I adore mine," Sara confessed.

"I'm really happy for you," Lori said, sincerely meaning it.

Sara looked nothing like the farmwives that used to shop in town when Lori was young. She was wearing low-cut white jeans with a zebra-striped top, which went well with her sleek red bob and arched eyebrows. When she wasn't busy being a wife and mother, she wrote children's stories and illustrated them herself.

"I've had only one published," Sara said when they both gave updates on their lives, "but I have high hopes. Here it is. *The Horse That Ran Backward*."

Sara insisted on giving her a copy of the book, even though Lori could think of only one child who might like it. She considered giving it to Joey, but Scott might think it was an excuse to see him again.

Would it be so terrible, letting Scott know how she felt about him? she asked herself. She knew he wasn't indifferent to her by any means, but her future was decided. She was going back to Chicago.

"You haven't told me how your date with Scott went," Sara said over cups of herbal tea.

"It was fine. We had a great dinner."

"You know it's not the menu I want to hear about," her friend teased.

"What can I say? We had a good time. We always were good friends."

"And you still are that? Just good friends?" Sara sounded a little disappointed.

"I care for him a lot," Lori admitted. "I always have, but I don't see a future for us."

"I guess there's a lot to be said for friendship." Sara didn't sound convinced.

"Is Sunny enrolled in vacation Bible school?" Lori asked to change the subject.

"Oh, sure. She loved it last year, and she was only three. Now she thinks she's a big girl."

Sara had gone out of her way to fix a lovely lunch of chicken salad with walnuts and green grapes and homemade rolls, but to Lori, having a long conversation with her friend was the best part.

"Wow. That sky is not looking friendly," Sara said as she loaded their lunch dishes into the dishwasher after a long visit, one that had lasted most of the afternoon. "Think I'd better check the weather report."

She flipped on the TV, and the two of them watched as ominous deep-red Doppler radar warnings moved across the western part of the state on the weather map.

"It's only a tornado watch now, but they may upgrade it to a warning soon," Sara said thoughtfully.

"You know, I really should start back, anyway," Lori said. "I'm worried that Aunt Bess might be walking home from school. She's lived in Iowa so long that sometimes she's careless about storm warnings."

"I've loved talking to you, but you're smart to leave now. Keep your car radio on in case they issue a tornado warning," her friend said.

Lori said goodbye, with a promise to get together again soon. She hurried to her car, feeling the tension in the air that preceded a storm. The clouds on the horizon were dark and ominous, and like most Midwesterners, she had a very healthy respect for what the weather could do.

Her car radio crackled with static, but she could still hear reports about the worsening weather conditions. She was only a few miles from town when Apple Grove and the surrounding area were upgraded to tornado warning status. School was out, but would her aunt take refuge in the building or try to get home? Lori was too far away to do anything about it, but a terrible thought hit her. Trailer parks were the absolute worst places to be if a tornado touched down. Would Scott and Joey be there yet? Did the trailer park have an adequate storm shelter for the residents? She remembered a friend in high school who'd lived there telling about a dank, old-fashioned storm cellar for the residents' use that scared her more than the storms.

She had to pass the trailer park on her way into town, and so she decided to stop by. She was seriously worried about the safety of Scott's trailer. She drove up the trailer park's entrance road and spotted Scott's truck. Parking beside it, she ran to the door of his trailer and knocked frantically.

Scott answered, holding a sobbing Joey in one arm and a flashlight in his other hand.

"I was worried."

"You should be. There's a tornado warning. We're on our way to the trailer park's storm shelter, but Joey is scared to death of it from the last time we had to go into it. You'd better come with us."

"How close is the storm system?"

"One touched down near Benedict."

"That gives us ten minutes or so. Get in my car. We can make it to my aunt's. Her basement is as safe as any place can be."

She expected Scott to argue, but instead he rushed to her car, put Joey in back, and slid behind the wheel.

"Buckle him and yourself in," he said.

She was more than relieved to have him drive. He went faster than she would have dared, while she tried to comfort Joey and keep her eye on the sky.

The streets were deserted, and there was an eerie green glow in the town which boded ill.

Like most of the town's residents, Bess never locked her doors. Lori didn't need to tell Scott the layout of the house. He parked in the driveway only a few feet from the side door that led up a few steps to the kitchen and down to the basement. She had both Joey's and her own seat belt off by the time Scott came to a stop, and it was only a matter of seconds before all three of them were racing to safety, Joey secure in his father's arms.

* * *

Scott took a second to get oriented, then led them to the southwest corner of the basement. Obviously, Bess had sheltered there before because an old couch with a threadbare flowered slipcover was there beside a small table with a radio, several candles in glass jars and a box of matches. He checked and found that the radio was battery operated and already tuned to the best station for local weather updates.

He looked around and saw that the only window that might be dangerous in terms of broken glass had been boarded up. Bess had made all the necessary preparations to ride out a tornado, but he wondered where she was.

Lori had her purse and a book with her, and she was urgently checking her cell phone.

"Thank the Lord!" she said fervently. "There's a message from Aunt Bess. She's staying with some of her students. They were working on a class project when the principal ushered them down to the boiler room to take shelter. That's a relief. My worst fear was that she'd be walking home when the storm hit."

"She could knock on any door in town, and they'd take her in," Scott said pragmatically.

"You're right, but it's hard not to worry about the people you love."

Did she suspect that the ones he loved best were here with him? He'd been so glad to see her drive up to his trailer that he'd nearly scooped her into his arms along with his son.

"Where's Petey?" Joey asked, his tears dried on his cheeks but his eyes still wide with apprehension.

"He lives in the garage," Lori said. "I'm sure he'll be all right."

"But what if the storm comes?" Joey asked in a panicky voice.

"You stay here with Lori," Scott ordered. "I'll run and get him."

"Scott, no!" cried Lori.

Scott caught a glimpse of her face, deathly pale in the gloom of the basement, but he didn't want Joey to come out of their shelter and find a dead rabbit.

"It will only take a minute," he said, bounding up the basement steps as the town's tornado siren issued its shrill warning.

He could go out the back patio door and be a few steps from the garage. It was a risk, but one glance at the sky assured him that he had a good chance of getting back inside safely.

The overhead garage door was down, but it went up easily. Even with the storm turning day into night, he could see the sturdy rabbit pen and its trembling occupant. There was no time to lug the heavy pen into the basement, so he lifted out the oversized fur ball and sprinted back to the house, not taking the time to close the garage door.

He was proud of both his son and Lori. When he got back, she had lit two candles and was reading to Joey from the book that she'd brought into the basement with her. However frightened she might be, she'd put Joey first.

He set the rabbit on the concrete floor, and it immediately hopped behind the couch. Joey leaned over the back of the couch to see it, then contently continued listening to the story.

When she finished, Lori looked at Scott with liquid eyes and asked in a hesitant voice, "Would you mind if we all join hands and ask God to keep us and everyone in town safe from the storm?"

Joey complied immediately, putting his small hand in Lori's, and Scott didn't even think of refusing. He took their free hands and completed the circle.

Later he wouldn't remember the words of her prayer, but he would never forget the sense of calm that came over all three of them. Outside he could hear the storm raging and knew that the house above them could be swept away at any minute.

Joey cuddled beside Lori and closed his eyes, maybe trying to shut out the frightening noise of the storm, as loud as a locomotive. Scott sat on the other side of her because there was no room beside his son. He leaned forward, elbows on his knees, and echoed in his mind her prayer for deliverance from the tornado coming their way.

He felt Lori's hand on his shoulder and leaned back beside her.

"Have you ever been in a tornado?" she asked so softly that Joey might not have heard.

"I had a friend who was a storm chaser. He talked me into going out in his truck once. Never again! And if you're ever caught on the highway when a tornado's coming, it's not safe to hide under a highway bridge. The steel and concrete won't collapse, but bridges are natural wind tunnels. You can be sucked right out."

She shivered, but Joey stayed quiet beside her, his eyes still shut. Maybe he'd fallen asleep because the mad dash here and the threatening storm were too much for him to process.

Scott put his arm on the couch, behind Lori, and was able to touch his son's ruffled hair. Joey didn't stir at his father's light caress, so Scott spoke directly into Lori's ear in an effort to be heard.

"I can't believe he fell asleep," he said.

Before she could answer, a terrifying sound was all around them, like a dozen massive freight trains barreling overhead. It was like nothing he'd ever heard, and he instinctively wrapped his arm around Lori. She was making little noises out of fear, and Joey awoke, crying out in terror. Scott gathered them both to him, trying to shelter them with his body and his will.

There was no way to know how long it lasted, but he'd never been so frightened in his life. Alone, he could have endured the tornado with a measure of calm, but he was desperate to protect Joey and Lori—desperate and helpless. It was the worst feeling of his life.

His ears had been so battered by the force of the tornado that he scarcely realized when the worst was over. Joey was on Lori's lap, and she'd burrowed her head into Scott's shoulder. When he turned his head, her face was so close to his lips that he brushed them over her forehead, tasting the sweetness of her skin and feeling the tickle of her hair.

He trailed his lips down to the tip of her nose and wanted to kiss her, even if the house above was ready to collapse around them.

"Daddy!" Joey shrieked.

His son, who'd been so brave in the eye of the tornado, started crying, letting out all his bottled-up terror.

"Joey, baby, it's over. You're okay. You were such a brave boy. It's okay now," Scott soothed.

He stood and picked the boy up, comforting him with mumbled words and stroking his shoulder to reassure him.

Lori stood, too, saying soft and reassuring words to his son.

When at last Joey's weeping tapered off to a strangled sob, he cried out indignantly, "I'm not a baby."

"No, you're certainly not," Scott agreed.

"You're a very brave boy," Lori said.

In the distance Scott heard the sirens of emergency vehicles, easily distinguished from the urgent wail of the tornado siren.

For a few minutes they caught their breaths. Then Lori prayed aloud, thanking the Lord for their deliverance and asking Him to preserve the lives of others who were in peril.

They didn't join hands, but he said a silent "amen" and tried to prepare himself for the destruction they would surely find outside.

How much of the town had been destroyed?

Chapter Ten

Lori followed Scott upstairs to the front porch, Joey still clinging to his neck. They stared in stunned silence at the aftermath of the tornado, broken branches and debris everywhere, and then Lori caught her breath and again uttered a prayer of thanks for their deliverance.

"That siren is a call to all the volunteer firemen," Scott said when she finished. "I have to go. Will you watch Joey until I can come back for him?"

"Of course." She reached out her arms to take his son, but Joey was reluctant to leave the security of his father's arms.

"Listen, Joey, you know what firemen do, don't you?" Scott asked.

"They put out fires and save people," said Joey.

Scott nodded. "And you understand that I have to go help people who may not be as lucky as we are. I'll come back for you as soon as I possibly can. Now, will you be a big boy for Lori?"

Joey nodded dubiously and let Lori take his hand when Scott put him down.

"Both of you stay in the house. There may be power lines on the ground or falling branches," he warned.

"We won't take any chances. Joey will be fine until you can come for him," Lori promised, wishing that he didn't have to leave.

She and Joey both watched as he carefully made his way down the street on foot toward the fire station at the other end of town. She badly wanted to go with him, anxious about her aunt's safety and that of the other townspeople, but she knew that her turn to help would come later.

Taking a worried look around her, she couldn't believe that her aunt's house had survived intact. A giant oak that had stood in front of the neighbor's house for as long as anyone could remember had virtually split in two, with only the jagged trunk with half the tree's branches still firmly rooted in the ground. Damage was everywhere. One huge limb was embedded in the roof of a garage three houses down on the other side of the street. As she looked in that direction, she could see that the destruction got worse the farther one looked down the street. She prayed that everyone had stayed safe in basement shelters and again thanked the Lord with all her heart for keeping them safe.

Joey sniffled, and she turned all her attention to him.

"Hey, how about you and I go find Petey? I bet he's still hiding behind the couch in the basement."

"Maybe he's scared." Joey clung to her hand as though it were a lifeline.

"You'd better tell him it's safe to come out. Maybe

he'd like a little snack after all the excitement. I think Aunt Bess has some nice lettuce in her fridge."

Joey gave another longing look in the direction his father had gone, then followed her back into the house.

Scott cut between houses to avoid fallen lines and debris until the neat brick building that housed the town's fire and rescue company was in sight.

Joey was in good hands with Lori. She wouldn't let him stray outside. He trusted her to distract the boy from the destruction all around them.

The farther he went, the more wind damage he saw. He wouldn't know where the tornado had touched down until reports came into the fire station, but Bess's house had survived miraculously well.

He wanted to be back at her house, and not only because of his son. He hadn't felt so close to anyone in a long time as he had to Lori in the shelter of the basement. There were so many things he wanted to say to her, but in the gloomy aftermath of the storm, he didn't know whether he would ever get to say them.

What would have happened if he'd kissed her? Would she be angry? He didn't think so, but it would have made life much more complicated for both of them.

He skirted around a green-striped awning that could have belonged to one of his neighbors and wondered how the trailer park had fared. For all he knew, he might have lost his home and everything in it, but that didn't seem important right now. As long as Joey and Lori were safe, he could deal with anything else.

The roof had been ripped off an old Victorian house just a block from the fire station, and he tried to figure out the path of the funnel cloud by the damage he saw. He knew tornados were capricious, capable of demolishing a house and leaving the one next to it undamaged.

As soon as he stepped into the oversized garage that housed the town's only fire engine, he didn't have time to think about anything but the rescue efforts under way. The fire engine was already out looking for potential hot spots, and ambulances from the two nearest hospitals were out answering emergency calls and looking for the injured. Half the men in town, along with a few of the women on the volunteer force, had congregated there for instructions.

"There's good news and bad," Bud Hawkins, the acting fire chief, shouted out. "So far no casualties that we know of, and the power company and the gas company have emergency crews on the way. We've put out an all-county call for emergency vehicles. The bad news is that the tornado took out some homes on Jericho Street and did some damage at the school, then leveled a house and all the outbuildings in zone three."

The chief dispatched all the volunteers' pickups, and Scott found himself riding with his best friend, Gary Planter.

"You see pictures on TV, but what a shock to see damage like this in your own town," Gary said, not sounding quite himself. "Thank the Lord that it missed our street."

Scott agreed, but he didn't have words for the way he felt. There was debris everywhere, and huge trees that had stood for a hundred or more years had been uprooted. At the Hastings farm, a place where he'd played as a kid, the house was roofless and stripped bare of everything but support beams and some inside plumbing, and the barn was totally flattened. The family car was lying on its side, totaled by a downed tree. Some neighbors were already at work using sledgehammers to take apart barn siding, which was blocking the driveway.

"Family's over at my place," one of the neighbors said.

"Any damage there?" Scott asked.

"Made a mess in our orchard, and I can't account for a couple of Angus, one with a calf. But thankfully, we weren't hurt. Didn't even lose a window in the house."

"Doesn't seem real, does it?" another said, a farmhand whom Scott didn't recognize.

Scott shook his head and went over to help clear the dirt track that led to what had once been the house. He was glad to have hard physical labor to take his mind away from what could have happened. What if he and Joey had been outside when the tornado hit? What if Bess's house had been destroyed above them? Would the basement shelter have been enough to keep them safe?

His stomach clenched and icy fingers of fear rippled down his spine at the thought of losing his son—and Lori. There might not be a future for them together, but the danger they'd shared made him realize that he loved her even more than when they were younger.

For the first time in a very long time, he wanted to cry, both for the farm family that had lost everything and for the bleak future he faced without Lori.

The power was off, and an unnatural twilight enveloped the house. Joey stayed close as Lori found matches and lit a few candles to bring a measure of cheer to the kitchen.

Armed with a flashlight, a dish of water and a bag of ready-to-use salad, she and Joey crept down to the basement. They searched all the dark corners, without finding the rabbit. Joey's heart wasn't in it. He wanted to go back upstairs, and she was more than willing, but for a different reason. Joey was scared of the place where they'd taken refuge from the storm. She was afraid of the memory of Scott sheltering them both in his arms.

Remembering how close he'd come to kissing her, she felt weak. It would have changed everything. She wouldn't be able to pretend that they were just old friends who had happened to cross paths again.

She followed Joey up the stairs, his little legs already losing the chubbiness of a toddler. What if he slipped and fell? She put her hand protectively on his arm. Was this how Scott felt about his son? He was God's miracle, a child so lovable and full of promise that her throat tightened at the thought of never seeing him again after she left.

She couldn't revamp her whole life just because Scott had a beautiful son. What possible life could she have in Apple Grove? Scott might not be over the trauma of losing his wife, and even if he were, what future would they have together? She didn't want to be one of those wives who went to church alone, pretending that it didn't hurt to have a marriage without a shared faith.

They'd just returned to the kitchen when the side door was flung open, and her aunt breathlessly hurried up the steps to the kitchen.

"I'm so thankful you're all right!" Lori and Bess both said at the same time, rushing to hug each other.

"Joey!" Bess reached out her arms, and the little boy ran into them.

"Did you walk home?" Lori asked, concerned that her aunt didn't appreciate how dangerous it was outdoors.

"Oh, my, no. One of the other teachers gave me a ride," Bess explained. "We didn't see any lines down on our street, but this town is no place to be walking around. Now, I can't tell you how much work I have to do. Whatever did we do before cell phones?"

"What can I do?"

Lori knew that her aunt would be involved some way in helping the rescue and cleanup efforts, and she was eager to be part of it.

"Well, I've already talked to Reverend Bachman. We'll use the church basement as temporary shelter for anyone who needs it, although I suspect the homeless have already been taken in by neighbors and relatives. What we really need is to coordinate our efforts with the Red Cross. They're on the way with food, cots, blankets and first-aid supplies. A lot of volunteers are coming to help with the cleanup, and they'll all need meals and a place to rest. I'm in charge of the kitchen."

In spite of the seriousness of the situation, Lori had to smile at the thought of her aunt in charge of feeding people. She hoped Bess's recipe for pasta pudding wouldn't be on the menu.

"Of course, lots of the church ladies are coming to help. I'll be more coordinator than cook. Now, what do we have here that we should take to the church?" Bess started opening cupboards and peering into them with a rather rattled expression. "You will help, won't you, dear?"

"You don't even need to ask. Joey can come with us," Lori said.

"Certainly." Bess smiled with a warmth that children

could never resist. "I bet you know how to set a table, don't you, Joey? Put on napkins and knives and forks?"

"My dad lets me do it at home," Joey said proudly.

"Of course, he's a very good daddy. Right now I bet he's out helping people and cleaning up all the branches that fell down," Bess said.

"He's a volunteer fireman," Joey told her proudly, stumbling a little over the long title.

"I see your car is here." Bess was filling a plastic bag with items from her pantry. "As far as I know, there isn't much damage between here and the church. Let's load up everything that might be useful and get over there."

At her aunt's insistence, Lori virtually stripped the food pantry and carried the cans and boxes out to her car. Joey got into the spirit of things by lugging full plastic bags closer to the door and arranging them in neat lines.

"Everything in the fridge may spoil, so why don't you two have a little snack before we leave?" Bess suggested.

Joey had calmed down enough to drink a glass of orange juice and eat a bowl of cereal, but Lori was still too agitated to think of eating. It was the volunteers who would need good meals to recharge their energy, and she was thankful she could contribute something.

Never had Lori been more proud of her hometown. People streamed into the church, carrying cheese and meat platters, huge bags of canned goods and everything else they could manage on short notice. Everyone who'd escaped the devastation of the tornado was eager to do something to help. Because fallen trees or branches blocked some roads, a few farm folk even rode horses to the church, bringing donations of blankets, candles, and food for those who needed them.

Lori's eyes watered at the goodness of the people, but she didn't even have time to properly thank them, let alone give way to sentiment. Bess was wonderful with people but terrible with food. She had no idea what to do with all the donations that were streaming in, most of them in need of cooking or heating. It was a big relief when they got the go-ahead to use the church's gas oven. Many of the donors had brought coolers filled with all the ice they had on hand, and Lori used these to store some of the perishables that had been donated.

Bess urged the women of the church to put Lori in charge. Most of them knew Lori well enough to agree, and her first thought was to use some of the canned goods to make a big pot of soup. She put several women to work making sandwiches and a pair to work opening cans. She delegated the job of setting the tables to her aunt.

There was enough light coming in the high windows of the church basement to allow Bess to set up the tables, but once it got dark, they would be in trouble. Lori solicited candles from everyone who asked how they could help, but she wouldn't let her aunt or the other ladies light any until they were really needed. No one could give her any idea of when the power might be restored.

It was late evening when darkness made the cleanup effort more difficult. Volunteers gradually came to the church, tired, hungry and shocked by the extent of the damage. Most were in a hurry to get back to the cleanup, and their first request was usually for coffee. Lori managed to make instant coffee by boiling water on the stove. It was terrible stuff by her standards, but everyone gratefully welcomed it.

Joey had gone to the church's temporary nursery,

staffed by teenage girls, but he soon insisted on coming back to the common room to help Lori and the other women. The little boy looked exhausted, but Lori didn't try to discourage him. Until his father came, she was his security in this strange new situation.

By nine o'clock, the Red Cross had come, much to everyone's relief, and had brought cots, blankets and other needed items. Volunteers were coming in droves now, some bringing people whose houses were unsafe. Food disappeared almost as fast as the women could set it out, and Lori decided to make pancakes until the demand slacked off. They were the one quick thing that almost everyone liked.

At last Joey was persuaded to join the other children in the nursery for a sleepover. Lori profusely thanked the teenage girls who were watching the children. They were making the overnight stay in the church seem like an adventure, a terribly difficult job since some of the children came from homes that had been damaged or destroyed. Parents were out trying to salvage what they could or helping others clear away debris.

Volunteers kept straggling in for food and a brief rest, but Scott wasn't among them. Lori couldn't help but worry that something had happened to him. She wondered, too, whether his home had survived. Several of the trailer park's residents had come to the church for a meal, and their reports of damage weren't reassuring. The park hadn't suffered a direct hit, but wind damage was severe in some cases.

When there was a lull in the kitchen, Lori made her way upstairs to the sanctuary of the church. The pews were shrouded in darkness, but someone had lit two candles on the altar as a guide for anyone who wanted a quiet respite. Lori took a seat near the front and bowed her head in prayer, but at first her thoughts were jumbled. She didn't have words to express how grateful she was to the Lord for saving Joey and Scott and Bess from the storm, but she had faith that He could read her heart.

She did find words to pray for the town and all its residents, thankful that all their lives had been spared. She was only beginning to know the cost of the tornado in lost homes, crops and livelihoods, and she was still overwhelmed at the response from volunteers, some coming a hundred miles or more to help.

The prayer break did revive her spirit, and some of her weariness fell away. She hurried back to the common room, hoping that Scott had finally come for a meal and some rest.

Gary insisted that he and Scott go to the church for a meal. The word had gotten out a long time ago that everyone would be fed there, but Scott and his friend had joined a team working to rescue trapped and endangered livestock. Along the way they'd accumulated a half a dozen terrified and injured dogs in the back of Gary's pickup, and they'd had to drive to the next town to find a vet who would take care of them.

"I should check on Joey," Scott finally agreed.

In his heart, he never doubted that Lori would keep his son safe, but he still worried that Joey would miss him and be frightened.

"He's probably at the church," Gary said. "Let's check there first. I'm starving."

"Doubt that," Scott teased to lighten the somber

mood. "Not with that layer of fat you carry around your middle."

"Can I help it if I married a good cook?"

The electricity at the church was still off, but they easily made their way through the common room, now a temporary dining hall, by the light of the candles on the tables. An older woman that Scott didn't recognize in the dim light invited them to sit down, but first he looked around, hoping for a glimpse of Lori. His instincts told him that she would be here helping.

"I'll bring you some coffee," said the woman. "It will take a few minutes to cook up a new batch of pancakes. We're out of syrup, but I can give you brown sugar, jam or margarine."

"A little of each, please," Gary said.

"Just margarine," Scott requested wearily.

As soon as he sat, every muscle in his body protested. He didn't know when he'd been so tired. He hadn't felt this exhausted even when Joey kept him up all night with the croup.

"I'd better see if my son is here," he said.

"You can bet I won't move until I've stoked up on pancakes," Gary said.

Scott heard Lori before he saw her. She was talking to a woman standing by the kitchen door.

"What a time you picked to come home!" the other woman said. "How long do you plan to stay in Apple Grove?"

"I promised my aunt I'd help get the café started—if it survived the storm. Then I'll be going back to Chicago, after Labor Day."

"I think Main Street was mostly missed, except for

branches and debris flying all over the place," the woman said, returning to the topic that was first in everyone's minds. "If I live to be a hundred, I never want to see anything like this again."

"Chances are you won't," Lori said in a soothing voice. "Someone said it's been over forty years since a tornado touched down anywhere near Apple Grove. Something about the town being in a basin."

Lori hadn't seen him yet. Scott waited until the other woman drifted away to approach Lori, but her avowed intention of leaving Apple Grove hit him hard. Of course, he knew she was going, but hearing it after everything that had happened was the last straw in a long, terrible day. He slumped down on the floor, his back against the wall, and buried his face in his hands.

All he could think about was their time sheltering in the basement. For a brief, tumultuous period, they'd needed each other. If that was all he'd have to remember her, he would be satisfied. It was better than never connecting with her at all. At least he knew that he was still capable of caring for a woman, still open to loving.

When he looked up, Lori was sitting beside him on the floor.

"You must be exhausted," she said, her sympathy like a balm on his spirit.

"Yeah, but all I need is a few hours' sleep. Help is coming from all over the county, but there's still a lot that has to be done right away—livestock to rescue, unsafe structures to be torn down, streets cleared where falling trees have blocked them. Where's Joey?"

"In the nursery, down the hall and across from the preschoolers' Sunday-school room," she said. "Some high school girls have put down mats and blankets, so hopefully the younger children will fall asleep."

"Thank you for taking care of him. Sometimes I need to be two people."

"You're a wonderful father."

Coming from her, the words meant a lot. He tried his best, but sometimes he didn't feel up to being all things to his son.

He reached out and took Lori's hand, taking heart from her presence. As exhausted as he was, he had clarity of mind, which was new to him. He was beginning to understand what it meant to be part of a community. Maybe he'd been too stubborn about letting others help him. He remembered how church members had reached out to him when Mandy died, and wasn't proud of the way he'd retreated from their kindness.

Lori's compassion mirrored their concern, but with her own special kindness.

"Shall we look in on Joey?" she asked, pulling away and standing up.

They made their way to the nursery. Scott was pleased by the arrangement for the sleeping children. He saw Joey's blond head on the far side of the room and didn't try to approach. When he whispered his approval to Lori, one of the teenage girls shushed him.

"You don't know what a time we had getting them to sleep," the girl whispered.

"You've done a great job. Thanks so much," he said, deciding that Joey was perfectly all right where he was.

In fact, he didn't even know whether he had a home for Joey anymore. Was the trailer still habitable? It hadn't been a priority to check it when he saw the aftermath of the storm in the countryside. Until he knew what his own situation was, he probably should leave Joey where he was.

"When Joey Mara wakes up, please tell him his daddy was here. I'll be back for him as soon as I can," he said to one of the girls.

Going back to the common room, he saw Gary at the table, with an empty plate in front of him and a coffee mug in hand. He knew that he needed food himself but wondered whether he had enough energy left to eat.

"Scott, when did you last eat?" Lori asked, her voice soft and concerned.

"I can't honestly remember."

"Sit down. I'll be right back."

Lori came back with a big platter of pancakes and filled a plate for Scott, as well as serving seconds to Gary.

"I can't tell you how much I appreciate your looking after Joey," he said between bites.

"He's been a wonder," Lori said. "He helped set and clear tables, until I finally persuaded him to have some supper himself and go to sleep in the nursery. That's quite a son you have."

She brushed away a lock of stray hair, and he wished that he could see her better in the dim light. Her voice sounded as weary as he felt, and he couldn't even imagine how hard she'd been working, feeding the hordes of volunteers who had come from all over the county to help out.

"I can't thank you enough," he said, rotating his head to work some of the stiffness out of his neck.

"I love being with him." She sounded totally sincere, and then her voice became more impersonal. "I can't tell you how much help we've had. Everyone who's able is trying to help out."

Suddenly Scott didn't care about food. He just wanted to keep talking to her.

"Your trailer?" She seemed hesitant to ask.

"I don't know yet. No reports of heavy damage there, but a tornado is a freaky thing. It can flatten a hundred houses and leave one standing."

"Or pick out one in a neighborhood and leave the rest undamaged."

"Yes."

"Scott, I believe the Lord watched over us, protected us from the storm. I believe it was His hand that kept people safe even while the tornado was roaring through town."

"That and a good warning siren."

He didn't mean to sound cynical. He was just dead tired and still horrified at the extent of the damage. Everyone seemed to have survived, but there was no telling yet how many people had lost their homes, crops, livestock and peace of mind. After seeing so much terrible damage, he found it hard to feel thankful.

But Joey was all right. Lori had escaped injury and death. He suddenly felt ashamed of his attitude, but Lori had finished serving and was walking away without another word. He went after her, although his mind was fuzzy with fatigue and he didn't know what to say to her. He did know that he wanted to be with her and only her.

"Did you boys get enough to eat?" one of the church ladies asked, cutting him off before he could catch up with Lori.

He had a momentary flash of resentment at being

called a boy, but mostly he felt deflated and defeated. What could he say to Lori that would make everything good between them? What could he do to make her stay in Apple Grove—with him?

He mumbled an answer and went back to the table.

"Better eat your pancakes," Gary said. "I'm hungry enough to set a world's record."

Gary kept quiet after that, not asking anything about Lori.

Chapter Eleven

Scott couldn't remember when he'd been so tired, but there was still more cleanup work. At least his trailer park had escaped major damage, and he was able to take Joey home for breakfast, a bath and clean clothes.

He allowed himself a short nap after he dropped Joey off at day care, but he had too much on his mind to sleep for more than a couple of hours. When he did, he had restless dreams and woke up feeling drained and depressed.

He hadn't seen Lori when he'd picked up his son at the church, so hopefully she'd gone home to get some rest herself. She'd done a wonderful job calming and soothing his son. Joey was interested in everything Scott told him about the storm damage, but he didn't seem frightened or disturbed by his experiences. In fact, he wanted to go back to the church and help Lori some more.

That part wasn't good. Lori had given Joey comfort and security when he'd most needed it. He had a loving nature and had already grown much too close to her.

He'd be brokenhearted when she left, and Scott didn't know how to handle it. And Joey wouldn't be the only one with a broken heart.

Scott showered and put on clean work clothes, but his short break had left him anything but refreshed. The one thing he could be grateful for was an undamaged home. There'd been some wind damage in the trailer park, but the twister had mostly affected the people who'd made an effort to make the place homier. Outdoor awnings had been ripped away, and lawn furniture was scattered everywhere. Fortunately, there were no large trees down, so the residents could handle their own cleanup.

Gary picked him up to resume work, but Scott adamantly rejected his offer to stop at the church for a late breakfast.

"Let's see where we're needed first," Scott said. "I'd like to know how Main Street came through."

"Yeah, you're renovating the old café. How's that going?"

"Okay, I guess." Would Lori be pleased with the results? He'd have more enthusiasm for the job if she weren't planning to leave.

The business district hadn't escaped wind damage. The pharmacy's neon sign was hanging loose, an obvious hazard for anyone passing under it. Smaller branches and debris littered the street, and store owners were out trying to clear them away.

"Stop for a minute at the café," Scott said.

At first he thought the old building had escaped damage, but up close he saw a long crack that bisected the front window. It didn't seem likely that the glass would fall out anytime soon, but the window would definitely have to be replaced.

"Well, replacing the glass is too big a job for me. They'll have to get an out-of-town company," Scott told his friend. "Getting this place up and running is going to cost the committee more than they'd planned on."

He didn't want to talk about what it was costing him. Peace of mind. He had a feeling his life would never quite be the same because Lori Raymond had come home for the summer.

"We should pick up those dogs at the vet and try to find their owners," Gary said. "I know how worried my kids would be if they didn't know where our family dog was."

While they drove, Scott wondered again whether he should get a dog for Joey. Maybe he could give it to him when Lori left.

He sighed so loudly that Gary asked what was the matter.

"Nothing. I just need to finish the café and move on to other jobs. I bid low to help the town get a restaurant, but it's going to take me longer than I'd hoped."

"If you want, I can put in a word for you with my boss. Pay's not bad, and you work regular hours, except at the holidays."

Gary worked for a delivery service, commuting nearly forty miles to work every day and putting in long hours.

"Thanks, but it wouldn't work out with Joey. I can leave him at day care only from eight to five, and that's longer than I like."

"I hear you," Gary said sympathetically.

"How did you get time off to help clean up?"

"Took a couple of vacation days."

Scott smiled ruefully. The closest he came to a vacation was when he took Joey to his sister's farm. Then it occurred to him that maybe Doreen could be helpful. Joey could stay with her for a while and get Lori out of his mind. The less he saw of her in the near future, the easier it might be to accept that she was leaving for good.

He leaned his head back on the seat and closed his eyes, but he could no more nap in the truck than he had at home. There was too much to do and too much to think about. He was so tense that he didn't even realize his fists were clenched. He wanted to back out of the café job and take his son to a place where he wouldn't be hurt, where neither of them would be hurt.

Gary said something, but Scott had to ask him to repeat it. His mind had been far away from the tasks at hand.

Bess insisted that Lori go home to get some rest.

"We won't have to feed as many this evening, and there's plenty of help now that the roads are clear and the power's back on."

"I'll leave after we're set for dinner."

Lori couldn't remember when she'd been so tired, but there was always the chance Scott might come back to the church. Seeing him again wouldn't accomplish anything, but she was listening to her heart, not her head. She couldn't shake the nagging feeling that they needed to talk, although she couldn't imagine a conversation that would change anything.

"Leave, and I promise not to go near the stove," Bess said in a teasing tone. "I won't inflict my cooking on those wonderful people who are cleaning up our town."

Lori finally compromised, agreeing to leave after her

three Dutch apple pies were out of the oven. She'd had to use ready-made crusts, but she thought the volunteers who were still working deserved the best meal possible under the circumstances.

"Lori, I don't know what we would have done without you," Mrs. Jarvis said.

The usually staid church leader hugged her, and several other women thanked her profusely. She wanted to feel proud that she'd helped, but she was miserable.

She'd finally come to the revelation that she was very much in love with Scott and Joey.

She walked home, hoping fresh air and solitude would help put her feelings in perspective. Instead, she kept reliving in her mind the moments before the tornado touched down. She could still feel Scott's protective embrace, sheltering both Joey and her.

How long had it been since she'd drawn strength from another person? Perhaps not since childhood. She always turned to the Lord for comfort and guidance, and He never failed her. Certainly, He'd brought her home to Apple Grove after the dark days of her job loss. How could she reconcile these new feelings for Scott with the faith that sustained her?

Love wasn't supposed to make a person miserable. It was the best of emotions, a gift from God. Why was she so unhappy? What could she do about it?

A voice in her head kept repeating, Leave, leave, leave. Once she started her new job, her memories of Scott would fade, just as they had when she'd gone away to culinary school. Only this time, she didn't believe that she could ever forget him. Running away might not be the solution. Never seeing him again might be more than she could endure, but she'd accepted the Chicago job. It was what she wanted, a chance to use her talents and succeed in her career.

At her aunt's house, she hurriedly showered and got ready for a long sleep, but as tired as she was, she lay awake as dusk turned to full darkness, her cell phone on the bedside stand. She desperately wanted Scott to call her, if only to thank her for watching Joey yesterday. Exhaustion finally won out, and she fell asleep without hearing from him.

"The committee is wondering when the café will open," Bess said at the breakfast table.

It was the second week of June, over a week since the tornado had hit, and school was out for the summer. Lori wasn't sure what her aunt did during the summer break, but no doubt she would find plenty to keep her busy.

"The new window will cost a lot, won't it?" Lori commented.

"It's not just that. There's still so much to be done. I know Scott is working as hard as he can, but he does work alone, except on things like plumbing and electricity. Some of the folks have invested more than they can really afford."

"I hope you haven't."

Lori had no idea what her aunt's financial situation was, but Bess could be generous to a fault. As a single woman with an old house to keep up, she needed to be careful with money.

"No, I'll be fine, but most of the people on the committee are retired. They don't expect to make a lot on the café. That never was the intention. But they can't afford to put in much more."

"You need the café to open soon so people can start seeing a return on their investment?"

"Well, yes, but I don't want to put pressure on Scott. We thought there might be some things the men on the committee can do to help."

"He might have to teach them everything and spend too much time supervising," Lori pointed out.

"Yes, I've thought of that. It's a dilemma, you see," said Bess.

"Have you talked to Scott?"

"Not yet. I mean, he certainly wants to finish as quickly as possible, but we can't ask for a miracle."

Lori was beginning to see where this was going, and she couldn't—she absolutely could not—be a spokesperson for the committee.

"It was Carl Mitchell's idea," Bess said, trying to absolve herself of blame. "He thinks you're the best person to approach Scott, to sound him out on how long he thinks it will take to finish. Maybe tactfully suggest that some of the committee members are willing to volunteer their skills. Carl worked for the power company, you know, and another of the men is a pretty good amateur carpenter. He's famous in the county for his rocking horses."

"Aunt Bess, it's not my place to hurry Scott along."

"Oh, dear, we're not asking you to pressure Scott. I'm sure he's as eager to finish as we are. We just need someone to suggest tactfully that some of the men on the committee can help him. Maybe do some hauling or painting or some such thing. It will allow the committee to invest sweat equity and keep costs down a bit."

"But why me?"

"You could do it better than me. Otherwise, we'll have to ask people to come up with more money, and some just can't afford it."

Lori resisted for the rest of the day, making herself useful by cleaning out the clutter that had accumulated in her aunt's garage, but Bess wasn't going to give up. She was sweet and kind, but when she got an idea in her head, there was no stopping her.

"Five minutes is all I'm asking," Bess said over grilled salmon and fresh asparagus, which Lori had prepared for dinner. "Scott might welcome the help. He has a good reputation in the county. He probably has other jobs lined up."

Lori just shook her head. It wasn't that she didn't want to see Scott again. She wanted to see him *too* much, but that was something she couldn't explain to anyone, especially not her matchmaking aunt.

The next morning she decided to drive out to the Bennings' farm. She'd already talked to Sara on the phone several times since the storm, and she had an open invitation to come out anytime. They were one of the fortunate families who only had to pick up small branches and sticks to clear away the storm damage.

Besides wanting to see her friend, Lori needed Sunny's opinion of one of the test recipes. She'd made chicken salad sandwiches using pita bread. The chicken salad, which had ranch salad dressing, tasted luscious to her, but she had some doubts about the broccoli called for in the recipe. Would a four-year-old eat it mixed in cold chicken salad?

Lori's little car was parked in the driveway since there was room for only one car in the garage. She hadn't had a reason to drive it since the day of the tornado, and she remembered that the gas tank was close to empty. She put the container of individually wrapped sandwiches on the passenger seat and tried to start the engine. All she got were a few clicks from the starter, then nothing, not even a sputter.

The gas gauge wasn't quite on empty, and there had to be enough fuel to get to the service station. It was no go. She sighed in frustration. The last thing she wanted to do was deplete her savings on car repairs, but she'd need a well-running car when she returned to Chicago.

Aunt Bess came out the side door to shake out her dust mop but stopped when she saw Lori get out of her car.

"My car won't start," Lori explained.

"Oh, dear, you can take mine if you're not going far. I think of it as a town car."

Lori accepted her offer with thanks, assuring her that she was going only to Sara's. Her aunt's 1978 Buick was a legend in town, still shiny from frequent polishing. It spent almost as much time in the repair shop as it did on the streets of town, but Bess adamantly refused to replace the automobile, which her parents had left her.

"Tell you what," Bess said. "I'll call Alvin at the garage and have him come here to take a look. That boy never did learn to read very well, but he's a genius with motors."

Lori smiled at the thought of a mechanic who made house calls, but Bess was probably his best customer, not to mention his former teacher.

"That'd be great."

"On your way," Bess quickly said, "would you mind terribly stopping at the café and speaking to Scott about

using some committee members as helpers? The committee meets tonight, and I'd really like to give them his
answer about the volunteers."

Lori decided it was best to cave in to her aunt's re-
lentless demands that she speak to Scott about allowing
committee members to chip in with free labor. "Sure,
Aunt Bess. I'll stop by and mention it to him."

She supposed it was the least she could do for her
aunt, but she couldn't admit, even to herself, how much
the prospect of seeing Scott brightened her day.

Scott made a mental inventory of all the things that
still needed doing at the café. He'd hoped to get Sam
Jones to paint the kitchen cupboards, but it was his bad
luck that Sam and every other painter he'd contacted
were booked up through the summer.

Painting was his least favorite job, but it looked like
he was stuck with it. It was much more cost-effective
to paint the cupboards and shelves than to replace them,
but it was going to be a time-consuming chore.

He wiped his damp forehead on his sleeve, wishing
the air-conditioning unit would get there soon. With no
cross-ventilation, the building turned into a sauna on
warm days. The Weather Channel was predicting record
temps for June. Any way he looked at it, this was turning
into a really lousy summer.

"Hello."

He turned suddenly, startled by the unexpected voice.

"Lori."

"I brought you a sandwich to try." She waved a
Baggie in his direction.

"You made lunch for me?"

"No, it's one of my test recipes. I'm on my way to Sara's to have her daughter try one."

She looked around for a place to set the sandwich, but everything was too dusty. She thrust it at him, giving him no choice but to take it.

"Thank you." His throat was dry, and the words came out sounding like a growl. He added in a softer voice, "Very much."

"You're welcome. But that's not why I came by. It was my aunt's idea."

He groaned inwardly. He liked his old teacher, but he resented her attempts to play matchmaker. They were adults. She didn't need to make up reasons for them to see each other.

"It's committee business," Lori was quick to say.

"I know I'm a little behind schedule, and it's costing more than anyone had hoped. Everyone is so busy with tornado repairs that I can't even get a high school kid to help here."

"I didn't come to pressure you about finishing," she said. "The committee has a good idea. They have some retired people who would be willing to volunteer their help."

"Unskilled workers can be more trouble than they're worth," he said bluntly.

"You haven't even heard what they're willing to do."

He set the sandwich on a sawhorse and folded his arms across his chest. "Then tell me."

"Judd Horning has an old pickup, and he's willing to make trips to the dump. Carl Mitchell likes to paint. He did his own house inside and out last summer. Actually, Aunt Bess made a list of what people are willing and able to do. I'll leave it with you, and you can call her when you make up your mind."

She turned to leave, and his resistance crumpled. He could use some volunteers, and he'd be foolish to reject their offer.

"Lori, wait!" He cut her off at the door. "Tell the guys I'd be glad to have their help, okay? And one other thing."

"What?"

"I never thanked you for taking care of Joey."

"You know I was happy to do it. Do you think he's up to trying any more recipes?"

"Joey thinks a lot of you. He can't remember ever having a mother, and I'm worried that it will really hurt him when you leave."

"The last thing I want to do is hurt him."

She sounded so unhappy that he worried she was going to cry. It was all he could do not to take her in his arms and comfort her.

"I know. I know," he said quietly.

"You want me to stay away from Joey."

"Only because I think it would be best for him."

"And what about you?"

He couldn't answer. How could he ask her to stay in Apple Grove and be a fry cook when she had the talent and training to be at the top of her profession? What could he offer her? He couldn't imagine asking any woman to share his crowded trailer, let alone a woman he loved as much as he loved Lori.

With a blinding flash of insight, he realized that it wasn't just Joey he was worried about. He didn't know how he could stand to see her leave again. He needed to stay away from her to lessen his own pain. He didn't want to face the dark despair he'd felt when she left the first time, and he didn't want to remember his reasons for marrying Mandy. He'd tried to make her a substitute for Lori, and it had never quite worked for either of them.

"You're probably right," she said in a hoarse voice. "I can see why you don't want me to get close to Joey."

"I'm only saying…"

He didn't know what more to say. Helplessly, he watched her turn and leave.

Lori knew he was right. If there was no future for them, it was unkind of her to work her way into Joey's affections. Why did it have to be this way? She'd never found anyone to love the way she loved Scott. She wouldn't care where she lived or what she did if only they could share their lives in faith and love of the Lord.

She drove to Sara's, her heart heavy. It had been a mistake to come back to Apple Grove. Would leaving be an even bigger one?

Seeing Sara and her daughter did cheer her. There was nothing like an old friend to chase away gloom, and Lori had become very fond of Sunny. She brought back memories of when Lori was young enough to play with dolls. Better still, the little girl was enthusiastic about trying a new recipe.

Sunny left no doubt about her opinion when she carefully picked every last bit of broccoli out of the sandwich before she would even taste it.

Sara and Lori laughed. So much for that cookbook recipe.

Lori was sure she could come up with a more kid-friendly sandwich. In fact, she was yearning to try her hand at fancy gourmet dishes that would wow Chicago diners.

What possible reason could she have for staying in a tiny Iowa town that didn't even have a restaurant?

Chapter Twelve

Scott woke up with Joey straddling his back and waving a paper in his face.

"Whoa. Back off, partner. Let me wake up before you give me a paper cut on my nose."

Joey tumbled off, giggling and grabbing Scott's nose just as the alarm started buzzing. Scott turned it off, vowing that someday he was going to get a clock that didn't sound like a dentist's drill.

"What is this?" he asked, retrieving the paper.

"VBS, Dad. That means vacation Bible school. You said you'd think about it. It starts tomorrow, and I have to take this paper to Sunday school today."

"So you really want to go?"

"Sure. It's all about Noah's arch. We get to go to a farm to see animals. I can go, can't I?"

"I think you mean Noah's Ark—it's like a big boat," Scott said to give himself a minute to think.

He read the note and saw that the Bible school started the next day. Dropping Joey off in the morning and picking him up at noon would cut into his workday, but he didn't have the heart to refuse for that reason.

"I guess you could miss day care in the morning," Scott said, swinging his legs out of bed.

Joey could still go to day care in the afternoon, but he'd undoubtedly have to pay for full days. What he needed—and couldn't afford—was a nanny. Or a wife. But there was only one woman he cared about, and she was set on leaving Apple Grove.

Was he doing a good job raising his son? Some days he had doubts. He had trouble explaining the really important things to his son, like how to tell right from wrong.

"Can I go, Daddy? Please!" Joey asked insistently.

"Sure. It might be fun."

"You have to sign the paper."

Scott got up and rummaged in a kitchen drawer until he found a pen. He signed the paper but left blank the part where he was asked to bring snacks or chaperone the farm trip. He was willing, but a single dad just didn't have enough hours in the day.

Bess left early for church on Sunday to meet with the chairperson of one of her many committees. Lori knew her aunt was in high spirits because Scott had welcomed help from Carl and anyone else who had skills he could use. It looked like the café could open even sooner than expected.

Lori walked to church alone and found a place in the pew behind Sara and her husband. She whispered a hello, and her friend asked her to wait for her after the service.

Reverend Bachman's sermon was about the lost sheep, and Lori listened intently, wondering how it applied to her own life. At first she thought of Scott as the lost one, but wasn't she the one who was wandering off alone? Sometimes it was so hard to know God's plan for her life. Should she listen to her head and leave to take an excellent job or pay attention to her heart? She prayed for guidance, but there didn't seem to be a clear choice. She didn't know whether Scott wanted her to stay.

After services were done, Sara came running over and told Lori about her big idea.

"Not enough mothers have signed up to bring treats to vacation Bible school. So many work outside the home these days that it's a burden to expect them to bake. I wondered if you'd like to try more of your recipes for VBS. You could see for yourself what goes over well with the kids and what doesn't."

"That's a great idea!" Lori said. "I can finish the sweet treats and maybe bring some lunch entrées, like pizza or chicken crisps. Count me in!"

Lori was filled with enthusiasm for the first time in many days. She really wanted to fulfill her obligation to test the recipes. Her car had required some expensive work, and she'd need more money when she went to Chicago to look for a place to live.

After lunch she consulted the worksheet she'd prepared for the café, a way of keeping track of everything that had to be done before it could open. She'd arranged for the fire and health department inspections and found suppliers for everything from staples to free-range chickens and homemade pies. She had lined up two women to work as servers and a high school boy to work part-time as a dishwasher. She'd done a study and decided it would be more economical to hire a professional cleaning team instead of a custodian. A laundry supply company would deliver uniforms and towels. In fact, everything was ready except the café itself, and the volunteers were making a big difference in the timetable. The only big challenge left was to find a permanent cook and manager.

Scott wasn't expecting his sister, Doreen, but he was pleasantly surprised when she knocked on his trailer door Sunday afternoon.

"Aunt Dory!" Joey made a flying leap and landed in his aunt's arms.

"How's my favorite person in the whole world?" she asked, returning his hug. "You guys won't come to the farm, so I thought I'd come see what's keeping you so busy."

"Glad you did," Scott said, hugging his big sister, who was as tall and slender as he was. "Did you come alone?"

"Yes, I'm on my way to see a friend who moved to Missouri. You remember Gail Spencer."

"Vaguely. Remember, you're much older than me," he teased.

"Knowing how you cook, I brought some goodies for Sunday dinner. The cooler is in my van," she announced.

"Say no more," Scott said. "I'll go get it."

Joey chattered incessantly over a delicious meal of fried chicken, potato salad, homemade yeast rolls and fresh blueberry pie.

"I'm going to vacation Bible school," he said. "We're going to learn about Noah's arch."

"What fun! What's your favorite animal?" Doreen asked.

"Dinosaurs!" Joey exclaimed.

"I'm afraid Noah forgot to take any on his ark," she said, with a big grin. "But there's something for you in my van, if Daddy will go get it from under a tarp in the back."

Scott shook his head at his sister, knowing her generosity, but he was happy that Joey would have a treat.

It turned out to be more than either of them could have expected. Scott brought in a kid-sized bike with training wheels, and Joey was delirious with happiness.

"Now you can do something for me," Doreen said to Scott after Joey had entertained himself by sitting on the bike in the living area of the trailer. "I'm curious to see the café you're working on. I remember how much fun my friends and I had hanging out there when we were young."

Scott was secretly pleased to show off the work he'd done at the café, especially since it was so far along, thanks to his enthusiastic volunteers. Doreen insisted on going in her van, so he transferred Joey's car seat and they went into town.

Lori was curious to see how the café looked, especially since Bess had raved about how nicely it was shaping up. What better time to drop by than when no one was working there? She set out on foot, enjoying the short walk even though the day was humid and warm.

There was an unfamiliar vehicle parked in front, a dark van that she couldn't remember seeing before. She took out the key she'd borrowed from her aunt, but when she went to use it, she discovered that the door to the café was already unlocked. Before she could decide whether it was prudent to go inside, she heard a squeal of pleasure and saw Joey opening the door for her.

Scott had a woman with him, and it took a minute

before Lori recognized his sister. Doreen. Her hair was darker than Scott's, and her high cheekbones and square chin made her look more severe than her brother. But she had the same warm blue eyes and classical features that made Scott so attractive.

"Dory, you remember Lori Raymond. She's here visiting her aunt," said Scott.

"The Raymond who taught at the school?" Doreen asked. "She was my favorite teacher."

"The very same," Lori answered. "I just dropped in to see how things were going here."

"As you can see," Scott said, gesturing, "pretty well."

It was an understatement. The new paneling had a warm buttery glow, and the floor had the look of expensive tile, not linoleum. The tin ceiling had been repainted, making the whole place much lighter, and taking out the wall to put in a counter for orders had been a super idea of Scott's.

"Where are you living now?" Doreen asked while Joey investigated the kitchen.

"At my aunt's temporarily, but I'll be going back to Chicago soon for a chef's job," Lori replied.

"That sounds interesting. I seem to remember you and Scott were good friends in high school. Are you still single?" Doreen asked.

Scott clenched his teeth to stifle a groan. The last thing he wanted was his sister's matchmaking. Not with Lori. Please, not with Lori, he thought.

"Still single," Lori said.

At least she didn't look as uncomfortable as he felt.

"I keep telling Scott he should get out more, have a social life of his own. I know it's hard with Joey, but all work and no play isn't good for anyone," Doreen said.

What is she doing? Scott thought. Wasn't it enough that Bess had been trying to push them together all summer? And Carl, one of his volunteer helpers, had gone on and on about what a nice woman Lori was. Now his own sister had plunged into the fray, single-minded in her efforts to see him remarried.

"How long will you be in Apple Grove?" Doreen went on. "There's not much social life here, but I'm sure Scott knows all the places to go. He was a pretty wild kid when he was younger, but I'm so pleased that he's become such a wonderful dad."

"He is a very good father," Lori agreed.

"Would you like to see the kitchen?" Scott asked to free her from Doreen's inquisition.

"Yes, please," Lori said.

He was rewarded by her sigh of pleasure when she saw how the dingy little kitchen had been transformed into a clean, efficient work area.

"The steps are safe now, too," he said, opening the door to the cellar. "The volunteers painted the walls and shelves white and installed better lighting. You'll be perfectly safe if you need to go down there."

"Why would she need to do that?" Doreen asked, turning her attention from Joey.

"I'm going to help open the café," Lori explained.

"You'll be here quite a while, then?" Doreen quizzed.

Scott groaned to himself, wishing his sister would stop talking. He looked over at Lori, who gazed back at him, a shy smile on her face.

"The café looks great, Scott," Lori said, inching

toward the front door. "I never dreamed the old place could look so nice."

"Thanks, but you deserve credit, too. You've had a lot of input," he replied.

She laughed lightly, patted Joey on the head and made her escape. Scott had a lot to say to his sister if she stayed until after Joey was asleep.

"This is going to be fun," Lori told her aunt on the first day of VBS.

She'd spent the previous evening baking chocolate-chip oatmeal cookies, one of the test recipes. She wanted to start with something the children were sure to like.

After her visit to the café, she hadn't known whether to be offended or flattered by Doreen's attempt at match-making. She could tell Scott had been embarrassed. No man liked to be coerced into asking someone on a date.

She packed up her cookies and took them to the church in time for the children's snack break. Several mothers, including Sara, had volunteered to help, and everything went as smoothly as she'd hoped. Her cookies got rave reviews from all the children who ate them.

Joey energetically vied for her attention when she passed out the cookies, but she tried not to single him out for special attention. She was afraid he was be-coming too attached to her, and she worried he'd be hurt when she left.

Then Lori learned that the woman in charge of the Bible school, Annie Forester, was going to open a new day-care center as soon as she was done with VBS. She'd been planning it for some time, and Lori thought it was a wonderful idea.

The church council had agreed to rent out the nursery room during the week for a faith-based day care with an emphasis on Christian values. Annie planned to offer the children much more than just babysitting.

"I never saw a woman who was so crazy about little ones," Sara said.

"She radiates love," Lori observed. "Her own children are all grown up, aren't they?"

"Yes, and they've moved away. She's been a widow for four, maybe five years now, so this will be a new lease on life for her," Sara explained. "I'm going to help her out for the first few weeks. She can afford only one helper, so it may be a little hectic until she gets organized."

"I could come at snack time," Lori offered, surprised at how much she wanted to be a bigger part of the church community. She would miss the Apple Grove congregation something awful when she went back to Chicago. How could she stand to leave?

Joey was eager to get to Bible school every morning and was full of chatter about what happened each day. He especially talked nonstop about Noah's Ark. Scott had to smile at all the questions he brought home, but some were tough to answer.

"Why did Noah only take two animals?" Joey asked one morning over cereal.

"Two of each kind," Scott reminded him.

"What if some of the mommy and daddy animals had babies?"

"Maybe Noah counted only the grown-up animals."

Joey frowned, as though he were weighing his dad's answer.

His questions never ceased. What does God look like? Why can't we see Him? Why did God make bad animals like rattlesnakes?

"Can we go to the picnic?"

There was a question Scott could answer.

"Sure. It sounds like fun."

Bible school always ended with a picnic on the last day, a tradition from the time Scott was Joey's age. It was a potluck, but he figured he could pick up something ready-made at the grocery store to contribute.

Picnic day came, and they were among the last to arrive because Scott had returned to the trailer to shower and change. He could tell as soon as he got there that the children were very excited. There was a brightly striped tent with long paper-covered tables, a real boon since early evening in Iowa was still sizzling hot. The church had furnished hot dogs, buns and beverages, but the food table practically groaned under the weight of the potluck dishes. Scott put his store-bought apple pie on the table and walked away.

Scott was so proud of Joey, who was going to receive an award for perfect attendance at VBS. And though he tried to deny it, Scott hoped he'd get to see Lori there. He hadn't seen her since the unfortunate meeting with his sister. He looked around the picnic area, but he didn't see her. He tried not to lose hope.

When the time came for the VBS picnic, Lori was nervous. She fervently hoped that Scott had come with Joey, but she didn't know what she'd say to him when she saw him. It seemed like ages ago since they'd had a conversation alone, and she'd missed him. Thought about him—and Joey—all the time. She prayed she'd see him again soon.

When she went to find a seat at one of the tables, there was one place left—right across from Scott and Joey.

"Hi, Joey. Did you find some good things to eat?" she asked.

Joey's mouth was full, but he nodded happily.

She'd put aside her recipe testing and brought a big pan of macaroni and cheese, one thing that children always seemed to love. She was gratified to see that Joey's plate had a generous serving of it.

"Lori."

The way Scott said her name made her feel weak in the knees. How could anyone put so much feeling into one word?

Scott had cleaned up before coming, not that she wouldn't have welcomed him directly from work. He was hatless, and his dark blond hair brushed against his forehead and curled over his ears. She expected that it was a bit long because he didn't have time to go to the barber. This was the first time this summer she'd seen him in shorts and a T-shirt, and he seemed thinner. She kept her eyes focused on his left shoulder. She didn't need to see his deep blue eyes to know that they were searching her face.

"Glad you could come to the picnic. Joey did a great job in VBS," she said.

"Didn't you think I'd come?" Scott asked.

"I didn't…I didn't give it any thought," she told him.

"It's not like you to lie," he teased.

"Actually, I was afraid you would," she confessed. She spoke impulsively, but it was the truth. She didn't know whether they could be friends anymore, at least not the way they'd once been. She cared too much to go backward.

Suddenly, Joey looked up from his dinner, frowned at his dad, then Lori.

"Dad thinks you're awesome." He said it matter-of-factly and went back to eating.

"Where did you hear something like that?" Scott asked, reprimanding him. "That's no way to talk in front of Lori."

"Aunt Dory said so," Joey said defensively, wiping his mouth with the back of his hand.

Scott's and Lori's eyes met. She smiled and he shook his head, breaking into a broad smile himself.

She was awestruck at the way their thoughts meshed without words.

"Out of the mouths of babes," Scott said, giving her a look that made her glow with happiness.

Chapter Thirteen

"I don't go to that other day care anymore," Joey happily announced when Lori saw him playing with a model of Noah's Ark in the nursery room on the first day of the new day care at church.

Annie's day care had opened with sixteen children signed up as regulars and prospects for increasing the enrollment when she'd trained more helpers.

Lori was delighted to see that Joey was one of them. She'd come by only to help at lunchtime, but she enjoyed being with the children so much that she stayed until it was nearly time for parents to start collecting their kids.

Each day she spent more and more time with the children, happy to be a volunteer. She had plenty of time on her hands until the café opened, since she'd already sent the results of her recipe testing to Maggie, her author friend. It was fun to be part of the fledgling day care. She had nothing but admiration for the way Annie kept the little ones in a routine and still managed to stimulate their imaginations and teach them faith-based lessons.

By the end of the week, though, Lori had to spend time at the café to receive deliveries and begin training her two inexperienced servers. The new dishwasher had a leak, which she had to deal with. And the farmwife who'd agreed to make homemade pies was called away for a family emergency. Lori had to find a temporary replacement.

She hoped to open the café by mid-July, and the prospects of doing so were even brighter when Lori found a cook to work with her and take over the kitchen when she left. Carrie Hayes was a widow who'd retired early from working in the hospital kitchen. She lived with her older son on a farm a few miles out of town, but sometimes she felt that she was in the way now that her grandchildren didn't need babysitting. She was thrilled to begin work at the Highway Café, and her enthusiasm greatly relieved Lori. She didn't want to leave her aunt and the committee without a head cook.

Scott had moved on to a new job, but he did come to the café from time to time to supervise the last few details being done by Carl and the other volunteers. He never seemed to have time to say more than a few words to her, though, before he hurried out the door.

Things were going so well that Lori knew she should be happy.

But she wasn't.

There was an emptiness in her life, which her busy days just couldn't fill. She was in love with Scott. But he didn't seem to return her love. One morning she was in the café kitchen with Carrie, comparing recipes.

This was a special day, a rehearsal for the grand opening next week. Lori had invited the volunteers who'd worked on the café's renovation to come for a trial luncheon, and of course, Scott was included. It would give her a chance to work with Carrie in the kitchen and get some feedback from the investors.

"You gotta have a pork tenderloin sandwich," the older woman said.

She was wearing a cotton print dress, with a big white bib apron tied around her ample middle and a head scarf tied at the back of her neck. She'd asked Lori whether she needed to wear a uniform like one of the tan-and-white ones that had been delivered for the servers.

"It's up to you," Lori had said.

She liked Carrie's old-fashioned style and thought it was perfect for the kind of café they were opening. Carrie looked like someone's granny, a pleasant image that evoked memories of holiday dinners and home cooking.

They were trying out a few of the recipes that would be featured on the menu. Carrie was pounding the pork cutlets to make them thin and to tenderize them, while Lori was preparing the bread crumb and black pepper mixture and making an egg wash, which consisted of one egg and two tablespoons of milk.

"The trick is to coat the cutlet with flour, dip it in the crumbs, then in the egg and then in the crumbs again. The more times, the better," Carrie said, preparing the pork cutlets with expert hands.

Lori fried the cutlets in hot oil in a large skillet until they were nicely browned. When the café opened, they would be served on a bun, with mashed potatoes on the side, and, of course, smothered with chicken gravy.

"That will bring the boys running from miles around," Carrie said, with satisfaction, as she sampled one of the cutlets.

At exactly noon, six men came into the café, boisterous and laughing, and sat down at the lunch counter. Lori and Carrie would be serving them, and they already had generous helpings of coleslaw set out. The smell of fresh coffee and baked apples with dried cranberries and walnuts overwhelmed the plastic and wood odors from the renovation.

Lori was plating the food in the kitchen, putting as much care into making the food look appetizing on the plates as she would in a gourmet kitchen. These men deserved the best she had to offer. When all seven plates were ready, she started putting them on the counter of the convenient pass-through Scott had designed. Suddenly she realized one person was missing.

Scott wasn't among the eager diners at the counter. She was more disappointed than she could have imagined, but then her spirits lifted when the door opened and in he walked.

He looked tired as he took off his cowboy hat and hung it on one of the wall pegs. His eyes were shadowed, and his cheeks looked gaunt. It was the face of a man who wasn't sleeping well, she realized, and her heart went out to him. At least he'd get a good meal here.

"Scott, good thing you got here," Carl Mitchell teased, his white beard even fuller than when she'd first come to Apple Grove. "If the grub here tastes as good as it smells, we'd be fighting over your share."

"I think your wife keeps you pretty well fed," Scott countered in the easy way men had of joking with each other.

He nodded at Lori and greeted Carrie with a big smile. Carrie poured him coffee without being asked, a sign of hospitality in any good café, then went to get his plate. Lori followed her behind the lunch counter, interested to hear the men's reaction to the food.

"Oh, man, is this good," moaned Judd Horning, one of those who'd painted long hours to get the café ready. "If I didn't have a wife, I'd marry you, Carrie, just to have your pork tenderloin three times a day every day."

"If I were your wife, I'd put you on a diet," Carrie countered. "Nothing but lettuce and apples."

"You wouldn't be that cruel," Judd's friend Fred said.

"You have Lori to thank for the good eats," Carrie modestly said.

"There you go, Scott. Marry that girl, and she'll put some meat on your bones," Carl said.

Scott flushed but didn't come up with a witty comeback. Judd jumped into the fray, needling him even more.

"Now why would she want the town bad boy when she could have one of us fine fellows?"

"We thought you'd end up in the pokey," Fred said, with his mouth full of mashed potatoes and gravy. "I gotta say you're handy with a hammer, though. Remember when you nailed phony wanted posters on the telephone poles?"

"Rusty had it coming," Scott said.

"Probably," Carl agreed. "I'm still sure he knocked over my mailbox when you guys were in high school."

"No, I did," Scott confessed. "If you want, I'll put in a new one when I have time."

Carl laughed as though it were a good joke on him. "Don't bother. I have to admit, you turned out all right. You're a good daddy to that youngster of yours. Not easy to raise a kid on your own."

Lori worried Scott was uncomfortable with all the attention focused on him. She'd never believed that his wild antics meant that he was a bad person. Her instinct was to defend him, but she was wise enough to know that he wouldn't want her to. Men always joked around.

"What you need is a good woman to fatten you up," Judd said, dipping the last bite of his sandwich into the gravy. "Any chance of seconds?" he asked.

Lori grinned. The celebration for the volunteers was a success. Carrie went back to get another sandwich, and Lori's eyes met Scott's.

"What do you think?" she asked.

"I think the café will be a big success."

He'd eaten less than half of the sandwich and hardly touched the mashed potatoes. When Carrie began clearing away the plates, he pushed his toward her and stood up to go.

"Walk me to my truck?" he asked Lori in a quiet voice that only she could hear over the boisterous conversation around them.

She nodded and followed him outside.

Scott didn't know what he wanted to say to Lori, but seeing her there in the finished café, doing what she loved to do, brought home the reality of her leaving.

"Good meal," he said awkwardly.

"You hardly touched it."

"Guess I'm not used to rich foods anymore. But it was good, really good. The café should do a booming business."

"I was fortunate to find Carrie. Not only that, but she has a sister in Missouri who's on her own. She is cooking at a diner there and likes the idea of coming up here."

"That solves the problem of a second cook, then," he said.

"If it works out."

She would leave whether it did or not.

He smiled, trying to pretend that he wasn't living under a dark cloud of gloom.

"I've heard that you spend time at the new day care. I wonder how Joey is doing. He seems to like it. Is he behaving?"

"He's been a doll, always cooperative and ready to do anything he's asked. He loves to play with the Noah's Ark set."

"Yeah, he likes animals. I took him to the zoo in Des Moines last weekend. Joey wanted you to come along, but I thought you'd be too busy with the café."

"I haven't been to a zoo in ages," she said, her voice soft and wistful.

He looked toward the café to avoid looking into her eyes. There was a dark streak on the new front window.

"I should've cleaned that glass for you. Looks like a muddy handprint on it."

"That's okay. I'll do it or ask one of the volunteers. You did a great job on the renovation."

He shrugged. "It's what I do."

"So the zoo was fun?"

"Pretty hot, and Joey wouldn't have anything to do with renting a stroller. We didn't stay very long. The flamingos near the entrance scared him, but he got over it. I had to ride a camel with him—talk about a bumpy ride. And he loved the petting zoo. Made friends with a llama but didn't like getting his hand wet when he fed it."

She laughed, but it sounded forced to him. He hadn't asked her to walk him to his truck to talk about Joey, but it was the only safe topic. He wanted to take her in his arms and convince her not to leave, but he couldn't stand in the way of her fulfilling her dreams. Just because he'd given up on finding a better life didn't mean that she should. He appreciated Apple Grove for what it had to offer, and he was convinced that it was the best place to raise his son.

She reached out and put her hand on his, her palm soft against his work-roughened fingers. He looked down at her and hated that she was going to a huge city like Chicago. He'd never been paranoid about metropolitan areas, but he wanted to protect and shelter her. He wanted her with him.

He pulled his hand away. He was a realist, and Lori and he weren't meant to be together. That was all there was to it.

"I'd better be going. Take care," he said.

"Scott…"

"Got a garage to build. It's going to take the rest of the summer and then some to replace everything the tornado destroyed."

"Well, I won't keep you."

"The café is going to be a big success, thanks to you. Bye now."

* * *

"It's going to be the best little café in Iowa," Bess said, almost beside herself with excitement as she put the finishing touches on a sign for the grand opening.

Her friend Dottie was cleaning the front window with enough elbow grease to polish a diamond. Carl was using a push broom on the front sidewalk, and Carrie was humming to herself as she mixed the meat loaf, using Lori's favorite recipe. It was a combination of lean ground beef, ground pork and ground turkey, with oats instead of bread crumbs. It promised to be as tasty as the high-fat version that used to be served there.

Lori had researched diner food and decided on a sandwich menu that included loose-meat sandwiches, BLTs, egg-salad sandwiches and, of course, hamburgers. She refused to serve French fries from the freezer, instead making hers fresh. Hopefully, her healthier sweet potato fries, served with a low-calorie ranch dressing, would catch on.

She still didn't have a reliable pie lady, so she'd offer a crumb topping apple pie to be served à la mode or with a slice of cheddar cheese. As an alternative, the menu featured a fresh fruit cup with a dollop of vanilla yogurt.

Hopefully, her two young servers, Mary Beth and Shelley, would be able to handle the opening day rush. She'd already realized that a third server would be needed since they'd decided to stay open from seven in the morning until seven in the evening, which was possible only because Carrie was there to help.

Keeping track of everything needed for the big opening was a huge undertaking, but she was glad to be busy. It didn't give her time to think about Scott.

"There," Bess said as she came inside after taping the sign on the window. "I guarantee all the committee members will be here for the grand opening. I just hope you have enough food."

"We won't run out," Lori assured her, "although late-comers might not get as many choices."

Lori had just enough time to hurry back to her aunt's for a shower and change of clothes. She'd decided to wear her favorite black slacks and a starchy white chef's jacket, even though Carrie would wear one of her cotton dresses and bib aprons.

Lori was the first one back at the café, and she took a moment to enjoy the newly renovated interior. The soft butternut walls were set off by new wooden tables and chairs upholstered in bright red plastic. She'd chosen a few rural prints for the walls, although she hoped that local artists might display their work for sale in the future. She knew it was good food that would build their clientele, but a cheerful setting was important, too.

They were going to be open only from four until seven for the grand opening, but Lori had decided to feed everyone who came to the café by seven o'clock, even if it meant staying open considerably later. She wanted everyone to sample what the café had to offer and, hopefully, tell their friends about it. For now, word of mouth was the most important thing. The budget didn't allow for much advertising, and it was important to start showing some returns for all the people who'd invested in the café.

Almost as soon as she'd unlocked the door, Carrie was there, wearing a floral print dress in bright shades of purple and blue, with her trademark bib apron.

Shelley and Mary Beth looked cute in their uniforms, and Aunt Bess was on hand, in her best burgundy dress and a long, dangly silver necklace, to act as hostess and take charge of the bills for the big event.

Lori took a deep breath and hoped for the best: plenty of customers and enough food to keep them all happy.

She needn't have worried. By five o'clock people were waiting for tables or a seat at the counter. Except for a few mix-ups on orders, the young servers performed magnificently, and Carrie had an invaluable gift for sensing when they would run out of something. She could make chicken gravy faster than any chef Lori had worked with.

No matter how busy Lori was, she managed to keep track of the people who came and left. The one person she most wanted to come was Scott, but it was nearly seven and he hadn't appeared. Bess went to lock the door but allowed in the last two customers: Scott and Joey.

Lori heard Scott order meat loaf with mashed potatoes and fresh asparagus for himself and a fried egg sandwich with fruit salad for his son. Lori knew what Joey liked and made eggs in a basket, a dish that had pleased him when she'd first fixed it for him. She took it out and presented it to him herself.

"Oh, boy, just what I love," Joey said, bubbling over with enthusiasm.

"I thought you were going to miss the grand opening," Lori said, speaking to Joey but wanting Scott to know that she wanted them there.

"I had to work late," Scott said. "How did it go?"

"Great! We had a full house the whole time. Everyone was very complimentary. I have high hopes for the future."

"Do you?" Scott asked.

"For the future of the café."

Why did she say that? She didn't want to give him the impression that she wasn't optimistic about her own future. Her new job in Chicago was a wonderful opportunity. So why did she feel teary eyed whenever she thought about it?

Aunt Bess came over, beaming about the success of their first dinner. She put her arms across Scott's and Joey's shoulders, giving them a little hug that expressed her happiness.

"I'm glad two of my favorite men could be here for our grand opening," she said. "Isn't my niece a wonderful cook? I'm so proud of her."

"Carrie deserves as much of the credit as I do," Lori said, embarrassed by her aunt's praise.

"Some lucky man will snatch her up, you mark my words. Everyone knows that the way to a man's heart is through his stomach," Bess declared.

"Aunt Bess!" Lori couldn't believe her aunt had actually said that. Bess wasn't going to give up on her matchmaking until she saw her niece walk down the aisle.

"Lori is a great cook," Scott agreed. "That's why she needs to take advantage of her new job."

It wasn't at all what Lori wanted to hear from Scott.

"We like your cooking. You should marry my daddy," Joey said, with all the seriousness a small boy could muster.

"Lori has other plans," Scott was quick to say.

"That's a lovely compliment to my cooking, Joey." Lori swallowed to conceal the catch in her voice. "Thank you for saying it."

Chapter Fourteen

The café had been open only a few weeks, and already it had regulars. A group of town leaders who worked nearby came for a coffee break every day, pushing tables together and holding a regular town forum. The café did brisk business during breakfast and lunch, but dinner was a little slow. People still weren't accustomed to thinking of the café as a place for a night out.

Lori wanted to be happier about the café's successful beginning, but it was mid-August. Soon she'd have to give serious thought to when to leave and where to live when she got to Chicago. Her heart wasn't in the move, and she knew it was because she'd be leaving Scott behind.

She worried, too, about the need for a second cook at the café. Carrie's sister had declined to come since she had a gentleman friend in Missouri. If worse came to worst, Carrie assured her, she could handle breakfast and lunch but close for dinner. Lori doubted that the café could show much of a profit serving only two meals a day, but when she was gone, there was nothing she could do about it.

Carrie liked getting up early and cooking breakfast, so Lori came in to help at lunchtime and stayed for the dinner shift. That meant her mornings were free.

Scott hadn't been in the café since the grand opening, as far as she knew, and she yearned to see both him and his son. Her hours at the café allowed her to continue volunteering at Annie's day care, and she did so gladly, loving the opportunity to serve and be greatly rewarded by the time she spent with Joey.

Sunday was their one day of rest, but she and Carrie had worked it out so Lori also had Monday off and Carrie had Saturday.

On her Mondays off, Lori worked with the children at the day care until it was almost time for parents to start picking them up.

One Monday she volunteered to hang a banner the children had made in the church, partly so she wouldn't be in the nursery room when Scott came for Joey. Much as she wanted to talk to him, she panicked at the thought of seeing him. He hadn't made any attempt to call or see her since the grand opening at the café, and she didn't know what to say.

There was a place for banners above the signboard where hymn numbers were posted every Sunday. She carried a small folding step stool, hoping it would be tall enough to let her hook the banner's strings on the nails. She started down the aisle and then froze in surprise.

Scott was sitting in a front pew, his head bowed and his hands clasped together as though in prayer.

He was the last person she would expect to find in

quiet meditation, and she couldn't intrude on his private moment with God. She couldn't begin to imagine what he might be feeling or thinking, but she hoped he would tell her in his own time.

Cautiously, hoping a squeak in the floor wouldn't betray her, she backed down the aisle, left the step stool and banner, to be hung later, and hurried back downstairs to the nursery room.

Several minutes later Scott came in for his son.

"Lori, I didn't know you were still working here," he said, walking up to her while Joey finished playing.

"I'm just helping out on my day off."

"How's business at the café?" he asked.

"Breakfast and lunch are great. Dinner is a little slow."

Her answer sounded stiff in her own ears. They were talking like polite strangers, and it hurt that she'd lost him as a friend.

"Time to go, Joey," he called over to his son. "He's crazy about Annie. She's great with kids."

"She's brilliant with the little ones," Lori assured him, but she couldn't erase the image of his prayerful moment in the church.

Joey made a flying run to his dad, clasping his legs and talking a mile a minute.

"Ready to go?" Scott asked when he could get a word in.

"Can I come here tomorrow?" Joey asked.

"Sure. This is your new day care. You'll be here every day when I have to work," Scott explained.

"Lori doesn't come every day," Joey said.

"She has to work at the café. You remember when we went there for dinner," Scott reminded him.

"Oh, yeah."

Joey didn't sound impressed.

"Bye, Joey," Lori said, giving him a fond hug. "You were such a good boy today."

She watched father and son leave, hand in hand. It hurt terribly to realize how much she wanted to be part of their family.

Joey made a fumbling attempt to catch the ball, then was distracted by a yellow butterfly fluttering past. Scott grinned. Maybe his son would be a scientist, not an athlete like his father had been. He vowed never to pressure his son to be something he wasn't, but he did feel good about his decision to put him in the church day care. He wanted Joey to have a good start in life, like he'd had.

Even though he'd rejected the church in his teens, he realized how important his early grounding in the faith was. It was coming back to him now, the prayers his mother had taught him, the Gospel lessons in Sunday school and his parents' faithful attendance at church.

He'd first gone into the church to pray on impulse, but by the end of Joey's first week in the new day care, he had made it a daily visit. There, in the solitude of a holy place, he poured out his feelings to the Lord. He felt his faith growing day by day. Perhaps someday soon he would find the courage to speak to the minister about rejoining the congregation. Meanwhile, he had only one overwhelming regret: he didn't feel ready to share the news of his newfound faith with Lori. He didn't want her to see it as a ploy to keep her in Apple Grove as his wife.

Would she doubt his sincerity? He doubted it. But even if she rejoiced for his sake, she'd made plans for her life that didn't include him. He couldn't ask her to stay in Apple Grove when it had always been her life's ambition to pursue her career in a larger and more exciting place.

Joey threw the ball wide, and Scott had to hustle to catch it, making his son giggle with pleasure. He had a wonderful son. He had to remember that in the lonely days that loomed ahead without the woman he loved.

Lori continued helping out in Annie's day care whenever she had time free from the café. She admired the tall, lean, energetic woman more all the time. Annie kept up with the children with unflagging enthusiasm. Her helper, Emma, loved reading stories to the little ones and helping with projects. Lori did what she could and especially enjoyed helping the children make no-bake cookies.

Time was passing quickly, and she had a sense of accomplishment both at the café and the day care, but her nights were long and restless. She couldn't see a future without Scott, and every day her fondness for Joey increased. Sometimes she got up in the early hours of the morning and used her computer to search for apartment openings in the Chicago area, but she didn't have the heart to pursue them. Much as she tried to get excited about her new job opportunity, her future loomed ahead like a black hole.

She didn't know whether Scott still stopped to pray every day before he picked up Joey from day care, but the next Monday when she was able to help with the children all day, she felt compelled to go up to the church's sanctuary and see.

There he was, his head bowed as before. She waited

near the back pew, knowing Scott would leave soon to pick up Joey. She didn't want to intrude, but she had to speak to him. The familiar interior soothed her: the stained-glass window depicting Christ rising in glory, the organ pipes reaching toward the high ceiling, the dark wooden pews, polished by many years of use.

He rose quickly, turned and stopped, as if in shock.

"Lori."

"I'm sorry…." She couldn't think of anything else to say.

"You have nothing to be sorry for."

"I shouldn't have interrupted you."

"You didn't."

"Scott, I've seen you here before."

"It's okay, Lori. I've been wrong about a lot of things, especially turning my back on the Lord. I just didn't have the courage to tell you. I was afraid you wouldn't think I was sincere."

"Daddy!"

Joey came running down the aisle, followed by Emma.

"I'm afraid he got away from us," the day-care helper said. "He seemed to think you were up here."

"It's okay," Scott said. "But next time, Joey, you wait until I come for you. You know the rules."

"I'd better go," Lori said.

"Wait!" Scott said urgently. "Can I see you tonight, after Joey's asleep?"

"Yes, I'd like that," Lori said quietly.

Lori watched Joey and Scott walk out together, more puzzled than she'd ever been in her life. What did this mean? Why did Scott want to see her? She wanted to hope but was afraid to risk disappointment.

* * *

Aunt Bess left Lori alone for the evening after the café closed. Her Bible study group was meeting, and she proudly toted off an apple custard pie Lori had made for the event.

Left to her own devices, Lori was too restless to do anything but pace. She tried watching the news on television, without taking in anything that was said, then opened a book, without focusing on the words.

The last light of day was fading away, and still Scott hadn't come. She sat on the front porch, listening for the telltale sound of a car motor, but the night was so quiet that the town seemed deserted.

The sky turned midnight blue, and still there was no sign of him. Had he changed his mind? Lori said a silent prayer because there were so many things she needed to say to him.

Scott was still fuming, but he could understand his young neighbor's reluctance to babysit when her boyfriend was hanging around. When she finally called to cancel, he had to persuade his elderly neighbor to come over and watch his sleeping son.

He'd rehearsed what he wanted to say to Lori, going over and over it in his head, but the longer it took to get to her, the more he doubted that they were the right words.

The street was dark and quiet, but there was a light in the front window of Bess's house. He parked the truck and went up the walk, startled when Lori appeared out of the shadows on the porch.

"Sorry I'm late," he said. "My sitter canceled on me."

"Do you have Joey with you?"

"No, I found a neighbor to stay with him for a little while."

He walked up and took Lori's hand, guiding her to the old-fashioned swing that Bess still kept on her porch. There was just room for the two of them to sit.

"I'm glad you came," she said softly.

It was all the encouragement he needed.

"I'm not sure where I stand with God," he said, with a self-deprecating laugh, "but I think there's still hope for me."

"Oh, Scott, there's always hope."

"You've helped me to believe that." He squeezed her hand, trying to find the courage to tell her what was in his heart. "Lori, the last thing I want to do is keep you from making a success of your career."

"Maybe there are more important things," she said, so softly that he had to strain to hear.

"If you really want to leave Apple Grove, I understand. Sometimes I think of starting over someplace else, but it's harder for me. I have Joey to think of."

"Scott Mara, why are you here?"

"Because I'm in love with you!"

He didn't know what to expect from her, and her absolute silence made his stomach clench. Had he made a terrible mistake?

He went on. "I guess I came here to plead my case. I'm not much of a catch. I have a business that just manages to pay the bills, and Joey uses up whatever energy I have left at the end of the day."

"You have a loving heart, and no one could do a better job of raising Joey than you do."

"Lori, I've loved you since we were kids. I did some

foolish things, and I know now that I shouldn't have married Mandy. It wasn't fair to her, because she was always my second choice."

"Oh, Scott, I love you, too."

He'd wanted so desperately to hear those words that he could hardly bring himself to believe that she'd said them.

"If you want me to, I'll move wherever you go. There's nothing I won't do for you, Lori."

"Coming back to Apple Grove was the best thing I ever did. I belong here, Scott. I've tried to deny it, but it always comes back to one thing—*you're* here."

"Would this be a good time to ask you to marry me?" He reeled from the wave of happiness that washed over him.

"The best."

"Will you be my wife, Lori?"

"Yes. Oh, yes, yes."

She leaned close, her lips brushing his, and he gathered her in his arms for a soft kiss that left them both breathless.

"I meant it," he whispered close to her ear. "If you want to find a chef's job anywhere in the country, I'll come with you."

"You forget I already have a job, chief cook at the Highway Café," she said, with a happy giggle.

"You know, the committee is eager to sell the place. Maybe if we pool our resources and throw in some sweat equity, someday it can be your café."

"*Our* café."

"Our life." He still couldn't believe it was possible to be this happy.

"Will you pray with me, Scott?"

She took both of his hands in hers, no awkwardness between them. He wanted to thank the Lord for the greatest blessing he could imagine.

"Thank You, loving Father, for bringing Scott into my life."

"And Lori into mine."

His spirit had never felt so fulfilled, and the love he felt for her seemed to swell in his heart.

They sat on the porch, making plans, their hands and hearts locked together, until car lights broke into their solitude. The motor on Bess's aging auto stopped with a sputter and a gasp, and she got out without seeing them.

"Aunt Bess," Lori called out. "We're here, on the porch."

"Oh, my, I'm glad you called out. You would've startled me to pieces," Bess replied.

"We have something to tell you," Scott said, stepping out of the shadows.

"Well, it's about time. You two have been lollygagging on my front porch since you were kids," Bess said with a chuckle.

"You won't have to hire another cook for the café," Lori said in a teasing voice.

Bess sighed. "That's good news."

"I've asked Lori to marry me," Scott said.

"I hope she had enough sense to say yes," Bess said, never one to pull punches.

"I did." Lori hugged her aunt and then led her to Scott for another big hug.

"Congratulations!" Bess cried. "I had a feeling God had

something like that in mind for the two of you. He brought my darling niece back to Apple Grove for a reason."

"Amen," Scott said, a huge grin spreading over his face. There was no way he would ever doubt that.

Epilogue

"I've never seen a more beautiful bride," Nadine Raymond said as she watched her daughter twirl in a wedding gown in front of a mirror.

Lori smiled and let her mother smooth back a stray tendril of hair that had fallen loose when she'd slipped the gown over her head.

"Mom, I've never been so happy in my life."

"That's the important thing," her mother said with a broad smile, "but I still can't believe you're marrying Scott Mara. Why, I remember when mothers locked up their daughters when he came around."

"You're exaggerating!" Lori said, knowing perfectly well that her mother not only approved of Scott, but she was enchanted with her soon-to-be step-grandson.

"I am a little surprised that you're having the reception at the café."

"Mom, I've explained. The café is part of a new beginning for the town—and for my life. Anyway, Carrie has organized the whole thing, and she's wonderfully efficient. You won't be disappointed."

"It's your decision. I'm sure it will be fine," Nadine said.

Lori smoothed the skirt of her pale blue gown, a color that flattered her fair complexion and dark eyes. She took after her dad in everything but height.

Bess came into the room at the church reserved for the bride and her attendants. She'd put aside her preference for dark colors, which made her look slimmer, and was wearing a bright pink dress with a little white jacket.

"I have a little wedding surprise for you," her aunt said, beaming. "I've signed my share of the café over to you and Scott. I hope it's a first step to owning all of it."

Lori hugged her aunt, a little overwhelmed by her generosity.

After she thanked her sister-in-law for the gift to the young couple, Nadine went back to her worries about the reception.

"Do you think you'll have enough food?" she asked. "You've issued an invitation to the whole town. There's no telling how many will come."

Lori understood her mother's concern, but she had faith in the church's congregation. She knew there'd be more food than everyone in town could eat at one sitting, and she trusted Carrie to oversee the buffet.

"Mom, you've forgotten what it's like to live in a small town. It will be the biggest potluck in the town's history. Anyway, the only way to be sure no one has hurt feelings is to invite everyone."

"You're right, I'm sure," Nadine said, all worry gone from her face.

"Well, you don't want to be late for your own wedding," Bess said. "It's time for the bride to get upstairs. By now Scott should be waiting at the altar for you."

"You're right," Lori said, hardly able to contain her excitement. She wanted to sing and dance and cry out for joy, but first she had to get to the ceremony on time.

When Lori entered the church's sanctuary, she saw that Joey was standing at the front of the church, beside his father and Gary. She smiled at the intense look of the little ring bearer and honorary best man, who soon would be her son.

Lori hugged her mother and her aunt before they were escorted down to a front pew, her heart so full of love that she could hardly contain her excitement.

"Dad, do you remember what to do?" she asked in a teasing tone and was rewarded with a huge smile from her tall, silver-haired father.

"The only thing I want to know is when I get to take off these rented shoes," Doug Raymond said.

"Now, if you like," she said, hugging his arm.

"Your mother would die of embarrassment," he said, suppressing a grin.

The church doors were open, and Lori looked out with joy in her heart. Only God could have designed such a beautiful day for a wedding. The town's venerable maples had just turned a vibrant red-orange, and a faint whisper of warm wind stirred their leaves. The sky was a sapphire-blue hue that no artist had ever captured, and Lori's spirits sang.

She was going to marry Scott. They would become one in the sight of God. She felt blessed beyond words and ready to rededicate her life to the Lord.

"Her mother and I do. Her mother and I do," Doug said, rehearsing his line.

"Dad, you can't possibly forget what you're supposed to say," she said, squeezing his hand.

"Well, it's not every day I give away my only daughter," he said.

She smiled up at her handsome father, tempted to ruffle his wispy gray hair just to lighten his mood.

"I'm so happy for both of you," Scott's mother said, then took her turn being escorted to the front of the church, where Scott's father was waiting with Doreen's family.

Lori smiled up at her father, loving him so much that her heart swelled.

"Is it my turn?" Sunny asked, seriously waiting to do her part as flower girl.

Lori had opted to have only one attendant, Sara, and together they'd picked a lovely yellow gown for her, the perfect color for fall.

The church was nearly full, and it was time to begin the wedding. Sara's little girl marched down the aisle, with her basket of flowers. Sara followed. Then it was Lori's turn.

Lori's father gave her his arm. A warm feeling of peace and security washed over her. She felt in her heart that God had ordained this union when He'd brought her back to Apple Grove.

They started down the aisle.

Scott was waiting. Lori looked into his face and saw it was illuminated by love. He stood tall and handsome, his shoulders filling the dark suit he'd opted to wear in place of a rented tux. There was no hint of hesitation, regret or nervousness in his expression, only undiluted love.

The moment was lost on Joey. Several guests chuckled when he put the little ring pillow on the floor and poked his finger into Sunny's basket of flowers, no doubt curious about the contents.

"Joey," his father whispered.

Joey grinned, picked up the ring pillow and stood beside his father, his back straight and his face serious again.

Lori stepped up beside the man she was marrying.

Scott had never felt happiness like this, his mind, body and soul given over to joy. When Lori approached on her father's arm, it touched him like nothing ever had. She was beautiful beyond imagining, and he hardly dared believe that this wedding was really happening.

He would never again doubt that God was watching over him. He vowed to be a faithful, loving husband for all the days of his life and to never stop thanking the Lord for bringing Lori back to him.

He heard the words of the minister and spoke his vows in a strong, sure voice. Beside him, Lori recited her vows in a soft voice, but without hesitation.

"Now, Daddy?" Joey asked in a voice that must have carried to the back pews, judging from the muffled laughter.

Scott reached down and gently touched Joey's lips, but he could see his son's relief when Gary relieved him of the pair of golden rings. He realized that this was as momentous to his son as it was to him and silently thanked the Lord for giving Joey a mother.

"You may now kiss the bride," Reverend Bachman said, with a smile in his voice.

Scott became aware of the guests as people he knew and cared about, and a sudden shyness gripped him. He bent down to touch Lori's lips and was surprised by the burst of applause.

"Mrs. Mara," he said softly.

"Mr. Mara," she said, wonder, love and delight in her voice.

Scott took Joey's hand, and the three of them hurried down the aisle.

"I've never been happier," he whispered to her before they went to begin greeting family and friends. "I love you more than I can say."

"The four of us will have a wonderful life," she said, smiling up at him.

He looked at her, wondering if he'd misheard.

"My grandmother had a motto on her living-room wall. Christ is the head of this household."

"I understand," he said, taking her hand in both of his.

She felt a little tug on the back of her dress and turned to scoop Joey up in her arms.

"Are you my mommy now?" he asked.

"Yes, and I love both you and your daddy so much!" she said.

* * * * *

Dear Reader,

Thank you for reading Scott and Lori's story. These two shared a warm friendship that blossomed into love as Lori helped Scott accept the Lord into his life. I hope, if you are struggling with issues similar to those Scott faces, that you, too, have someone like Lori in your life to steadfastly help you on your path.

Throughout the years, I've been blessed with good friends. People who care about and nurture each other are truly gifts from God. Please take time to thank these special people in your life.

I love to hear from readers. Please e-mail me at: psharc@gmail.com.

Best,

Pam Andrews

QUESTIONS FOR DISCUSSION

1. Lori left her hometown in Iowa and worked as a chef in Chicago. She enjoyed the big city but missed small-town life. Do you live in a small town or a big city? What are the differences? Similarities? Would you ever move from your current home to somewhere completely different? Why or why not?

2. Lori comes home to Apple Grove to help get the café up and running. Have you ever had a time where helping others helped you recover your belief in your own God-given talents?

3. Lori prays that the hurt she feels toward the employer who treated her poorly will fade. She tries to be honest with herself about her own shortcomings. Do you struggle to be honest with yourself about your weaknesses? Why or why not?

4. Lori and Scott were friends as teenagers, but her unwavering faith and his rejection of that path kept them apart. What change in Scott's adult life opened him to God's presence in his life?

5. Scott's son, Joey, asks a lot of questions about his late mom, heaven and God. Struggling with his own lack of faith, Scott is hard-pressed to answer these questions. How does the reappearance of Lori in his life help and, at the same time, complicate his responses?

6. According to Scott, he and his late wife married too young, then realized they weren't meant for each other. Do you know anyone this has happened to? How would you counsel them?

7. What do you think the Bible verse for this story means in Scott's and Lori's lives? What does it mean in yours?

8. Lori uses her gift of being able to create nutritious meals to aid the townspeople not only in a time of rebuilding but in a time of crisis. Have you ever been called upon to aid in a natural disaster, such as a hurricane or flood? How did you help?

9. Have you ever tried to keep someone out of your life for fear of being hurt when he or she eventually left?

10. Scott comes to the realization that it's not enough to take Joey to Sunday school when he doesn't attend church himself. If you are a parent, how do you help provide your children with a moral compass?

11. On a lighter note, do you like to cook? If you were a chef, what kind of restaurant would you want to work in? Why?

Private investigator Wade Sutton plans to hightail
it out of Dry Creek long before December 25. The
town holds too many *unmerry* memories. Until
he's asked to watch over a woman in danger, a
woman whose faith changes him forever.

Turn the page for a sneak preview of
SILENT NIGHT IN DRY CREEK
by Janet Tronstad.
Available in October 2009
from Love Inspired®.

Wade wished he had never come back to Dry Creek. Or, since he had come back, he wished people hadn't been so kind to him. Barbara making that cake for him was putting him off his game. And then Jasmine— usually he didn't have any trouble taking a tough line with a suspect. But then, he'd never been tempted to kiss a suspect before.

He watched Jasmine's back as she walked to the table. She was ramrod straight and angry with him. He knew he'd come on too strong, but it was either that or forgetting everything he knew about law enforcement and refusing to believe she could be responsible for anything.

As a lawman he had to consider all the possibilities, and it was hard to forget that Lonnie had been her partner. She could have sent him a coded message that in some way had helped him escape from prison, or at least given him an incentive to risk everything to get outside.

He wished he knew how to look into the heart of a person so he would know what Jasmine was thinking. Was she as innocent as she looked, or as guilty as she had been the first time she was convicted of a crime?

He knew better than most how many ex-cons fell back into theft. He was often the one who took them in the second time around and listened to their sorry excuses.

"I gave you the biggest piece of cake," Barbara said as he sat down at his place at the table.

"Thank you." Wade smiled. It was the cake of his childhood fantasies, and he was going to have to force himself to eat it. All he wanted to do was take Jasmine home and then park his car at the end of the lane to her father's place. Why did she have to be tied up with Lonnie? Why couldn't she be a nice, ordinary woman like Barbara here? Carl never had to worry about arresting *her*.

Wade felt the smoothness of the cake on his tongue and the sweet tang of the raspberry filling. He smiled up at Barbara and thanked her again for the cake. The two kids at the table were smacking their lips and demanding more, just as Wade would be doing if he wasn't so troubled.

Then he looked down the table and saw his dear friend Edith. She wouldn't be happy about him keeping an eye on anyone. It was clear the older woman was very fond of Jasmine. That, of course, was the problem with being a lawman and trying to have friends. He liked things black-and-white with no shades of gray. He didn't want to have feelings for the suspect.

By doing his job, he was going to upset Jasmine and everyone else in Dry Creek. For the first time since he'd driven into town, he missed the barren feel of his apartment in Idaho Falls. He knew who he was there.

It didn't take long for Wade to leave the Walls' house, with Jasmine walking in front of him. The night was cold. Jasmine wrapped her arms around her body to keep warm and hurried to his car. He was still nursing that leg of his, so he went more slowly than she did. He made it in good time, though, and as he opened the car door for her, she nodded her thanks and slid into the passenger seat.

The first thing Wade did after he got into the car was to move the dial up on the heater. Snowflakes were just starting to fall, but they were scattered enough that he could clear them away with his windshield wipers.

He silently turned his car around and started down the sheriff's lane. The car lights shone on the falling snow, making the flakes look like pinpricks in the darkness.

"You don't think Lonnie would do something to my father, do you?" Jasmine asked. She looked up at him with eyes full of worry. "Lonnie's not very stable. I wouldn't want anyone around here to be hurt by him."

Wade shrugged. "With all you'd inherit if Elmer were out of the picture—"

Jasmine gasped. "I don't care about the money."

"Lonnie might."

That turned her quiet. He didn't want her to worry, though.

"He won't even have the chance to get close to anyone," Wade assured her. "We'll have the feds all over the place by tomorrow. Lonnie has a better chance of breaking in to Fort Knox than he has of sneaking into Dry Creek."

Wade hoped he wasn't lying. He had no idea what the feds would do. And they might have some completely different theories as to why Lonnie had broken out of prison. It might have nothing at all to do with Jasmine or anyone in Dry Creek.

"You'll be safe," Wade said as he opened his door.

He walked around to the passenger door and opened it. Wade stood by the open car door and watched as Jasmine pulled her coat closer to her body. She wasn't making any move to walk toward the house and he wasn't making any move to let her. Finally Wade reached out and touched her cheek. It was soft and a little damp. She must have been crying when she'd been huddled against the door on the drive out here.

"It'll be okay," he whispered to her as he brought his hand down.

"I'm fine," she said.

He nodded with a slight smile. "I know."

Wade had never kissed a suspect, but he would have done it now if he hadn't thought it would make Jasmine cry even more. She was barely hanging on, and he needed to leave her with her dignity.

"I'll be parked at the end of Elmer's lane if you need me," Wade said as he stepped back from the door. Snow was falling in earnest now, but in his trunk he had a heavy sleeping bag that he used on stakeouts like this. "I'll come to the door in the morning, before I go over to my grandfather's."

"You can't sleep outside all night. It's freezing out here. I'll leave the kitchen door unlocked in case you need to come inside."

"Don't leave anything unlocked. I'll duck into the barn if I need to."

Jasmine nodded.

Wade watched her walk to the kitchen door and go inside the house. Only then did he head back to the driver's door. He wondered if he'd get any sleep tonight.

He was losing his edge. The next thing he knew, he was going to be offering pillows to everyone he arrested and wishing them sweet dreams. When had he turned into a soft touch?

He waited for the light to go out in the kitchen before he started his drive down the lane. He already felt lonely.

* * * * *

Will Jasmine give Wade reason to call
Dry Creek home again?
Find out in
SILENT NIGHT IN DRY CREEK
by Janet Tronstad.
Available in October 2009
from Love Inspired®.

HEARTWARMING INSPIRATIONAL ROMANCE

Get more of the heartwarming inspirational romance stories that you love and cherish, beginning in July with SIX NEW titles, available every month from the Love Inspired® line.

Also look for our other
Love Inspired® genres, including:

Love Inspired® Suspense:
Enjoy four contemporary tales of intrigue and romance every month.

Love Inspired® Historical:
Travel to a different time with two powerful and engaging stories of romance, adventure and faith every month.

Available every month wherever books are sold, including most bookstores, supermarkets, drugstores and discount stores.

www.SteepleHill.com

Love Inspired

When widowed rancher Rory Branagan and his young sons find Goldie Rios sleeping on their sofa, they are tempted to let the disoriented car-accident victim stay. When her family heirloom locket goes missing, they help her search the farm. Soon they discover the perfect holiday gift—a family that feels just right.

Look for

The Perfect Gift

by

Lenora Worth

Available October wherever books are sold.

Steeple Hill®

LI87555

REQUEST YOUR FREE BOOKS!

2 FREE INSPIRATIONAL NOVELS
PLUS 2
FREE
MYSTERY GIFTS

YES! Please send me 2 FREE Love Inspired® novels and my 2 FREE mystery gifts (gifts are worth about $10). After receiving them, if I don't wish to receive any more books, I can return the shipping statement marked "cancel". If I don't cancel, I will receive 4 brand-new novels every month and be billed just $4.24 per book in the U.S. or $4.74 per book in Canada. That's a savings of over 20% off the cover price. It's quite a bargain! Shipping and handling is just 50¢ per book.* I understand that accepting the 2 free books and gifts places me under no obligation to buy anything. I can always return a shipment and cancel at any time. Even if I never buy another book, the two free books and gifts are mine to keep forever.

113 IDN EYK2 313 IDN EYLE

Name _____ (PLEASE PRINT)

Address _____ Apt. #

City _____ State/Prov. _____ Zip/Postal Code

Signature (if under 18, a parent or guardian must sign)

LIREG09

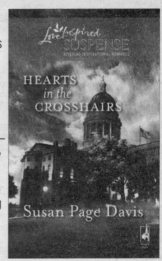

TITLES AVAILABLE NEXT MONTH

Available September 29, 2009

SILENT NIGHT IN DRY CREEK by Janet Tronstad

Private investigator Wade Sutton plans to hightail it out of Dry Creek long before December 25th. Until he's asked to watch over a woman in danger, a woman whose faith could change him forever.

THE MATCHMAKING PACT by Carolyne Aarsen
After the Storm

Widowed rancher Silas Marstow's young daughter and her best friend are determined to see him and single mother Josie Cane married. *Very* determined!

THE PERFECT GIFT by Lenora Worth

Disoriented after a car crash, Goldie Rios wakes up on Rory Branagan's sofa. All Rory's sons want for Christmas is a new mom, but is this unexpected guest the mother they've been longing for?

BLUEGRASS CHRISTMAS by Allie Pleiter
Kentucky Corners

Desperate to unite a town in crisis through a good old-fashioned Christmas church pageant, Mary Thorpe tries to enlist handsome neighbor Mac McCarthy. But Mac's a holiday humbug. Can Mary bring the spirit of Christmas into his life—and love into his heart?

SOLDIER DADDY by Cheryl Wyatt
Wings of Refuge

Young Sarah Graham surprises everyone by passing U.S. Air Force commander Aaron Petrowski's nanny inspection. Only secrets in her past could destroy the home she's built in his heart.

DREAMING OF HOME by Glynna Kaye

Meg McGuire has unwittingly set her sights on the same job and house as single dad Joe Diaz. Determined to give his young son the best life he can, this military man isn't giving up without a fight. But soon Joe is dreaming of a home with the one woman who could take it all away.

LICNMBPA0909